"Joram Piatigorsky's *The Open*  *and Yearning* are acutely observe into the surreal, the scientific, an their histories. The prose is precise ...characters surprise with their longing to change their lives, when they struggle to make sense of their histories, and when they find beauty in uncommon places and persons. I found the philosophical musings in these stories fascinating, as well as their implications for our future."

—Sergio Troncoso, author of *The Last Tortilla and Other Stories, Crossing Borders: Personal Essays,* and the novels *The Nature of Truth* and *From This Wicked Patch of Dust*

"The stories in Joram Piatigorsky's *The Open Door* are full of imagination, curiosity, and human longing. A lively, engaging read."

—Elizabeth Poliner, author of *As Close to Us as Breathing*

"Joram Piatigorsky audaciously weaves the fantastic with the familiar to show what love can do to those who yearn for it. Nothing is impossible in the worlds he creates, while the characters who experience the startling transformations that occur could be ourselves. Surprise and recognition are the hallmarks of these utterly original and delightful stories."

—Kate Blackwell, author of *You Won't Remember This: Stories*

"*The Open Door*" is a brilliant and vibrant collection of stories that spans the breadth and diversity of literary fiction, from grave to funny to poignant and all points in-between. It's this range of technique and emotional engagement that pulls the readers through each piece and leaves them anticipating what comes next. In a style reminiscent of Carson McCullers, Piatigorsky presents stories that are vivid with imagery while maintaining a dramatic element balanced by compassion for the characters. These characters truly drive each story to the point that you become one with the fictional dream that the author weaves so flawlessly. Even in being comfortably lost in the dream, you'll no doubt recognize upon reflection that you are in the hands of a master story-teller. If you take home only one short story collection this year, let *The Open Door* be the one!"

—James Mathews, author of *Last Known Position*; Winner, Katherine Anne Porter Prize in Short Fiction

"A beautifully written collection that covers the many territories between the real and the fantastic but that focuses on lives compressed by restraint and left desiring. A rich mix of art and myth, shape-shifting and wide-awake dreaming."

—Barbara Esstman, author of *The Other Anna; Night Ride Home; A More Perfect Union*

"Piatigorsky has sculpted a universe of desire, where a chance sighting can alter the course of a man's life, where even a pinprick of longing blooms into heated obsession. The characters in these stories inhabit a world that looks like ours but feels like a secret, parallel space, one where curiosity and yearning wander and flourish. Inventive, funny, and at times strangely prescient, these stories bring what Robert Bausch called 'the human news,' tidings from the heart in all its loving potential."

—Jennifer Buxton, The Writer's Center, Bethesda, MD

"Joram Piatigorsky has created an unforgettable mix of stories and colorful characters, including Inuit sculptures that spring to life, offering both surprising wisdom and comfort. The mix of humor and the universal angst of life's bittersweet passages propels the reader throughout."

—Sally Mott Freeman, author of *The Jersey Brothers*

THE OPEN DOOR
and other tales of love and yearning

THE OPEN DOOR

and other tales of love and yearning

Short Stories

by

JORAM PIATIGORSKY

Adelaide Books
New York / Lisbon
2019

THE OPEN DOOR
and other tales of love and yearning
Short Stories
By Joram Piatigorsky

Published by Adelaide Books, New York / Lisbon
adelaidebooks.org

Editor-in-Chief
Stevan V. Nikolic

For information, please email Adelaide Books
at info@adelaidebooks.org

or write to:

Adelaide Books
244 Fifth Ave. Suite D27
New York, NY, 10001

ISBN-10: 1-950437-04-3
ISBN-13: 978-1-950437-04-7

Printed in the United States of America

To Robert Bausch (1945 – 2018), author,

devoted teacher and messenger from the heart

Bob (left) and I at Joyce Maynard's writing workshop
in Lake Atitlan, Guatemala, 2008

Contents

Foreword

In 1996, when I was fully engaged in research at the National Institutes of Health and Chief of the Laboratory of Molecular and Developmental Biology, National Eye Institute, I wrote my very first, very short story. It was three pages. Lona and I were on summer vacation strolling along a wooded path overlooking a peaceful bay in Maine on a beautiful, sunny day. I'd dabbled at writing in college, where I took a number of literature courses, and for a long time wanted to express myself in writing. Science, however, stole my time to do so.

"If not now, when?" I asked myself.

Lona took out her sketchpad and I leaned against a tree in the forest and started writing whatever came to my mind. Since I was collecting Inuit art, I wrote about a teenage Inuit boy who went hunting for caribou with another boy his age who was visiting the Arctic. They killed a caribou, and I was totally involved in their adventure. I had created a fictional world on paper that was as real for me as the ground I was sitting on. I decided to use the free cracks of time I had in science, and there were not many, to write. Being a novice and badly in need of learning how to write non-science, I took a series of workshops in fiction at The Writer's Center in Bethesda.

After excellent workshops by Kate Blackwell and Elizabeth Poliner, I took several with Robert (Bob) Bausch. In addition to his infectious enthusiasm and knowledge, he always encouraged me as I struggled to learn the skills of writing. He never laughed at my mixed metaphors, or belittled my clumsy efforts at satire, or ridiculed my occasional runaway fantasies. He always found the few sentences that glowed for him – he pointed to the pony under the dung – and I kept writing.

I thank Barbara Esstman (whose workshop on novels and memoirs I also took), Mía R. García and Lucy Chumbley for excellent editing, and Margaret Dimond for constructive suggestions and continuous help along the way. As usual, my wife Lona always had valuable input and encouragement.

Ismael Carrillo did all the illustrations. I am grateful to Stevan V. Nikolic and Adelaide Books for support in publishing these stories.

The Miracle of Estelle was published in the April 2018 issue of Adelaide Literary Magazine.

Each story was written independently over a number of years without any thought to link them. When I reread this collection, however, it was a revelation to me how much the theme of love and yearning were woven throughout each story. I discovered that is one of the most remarkable and unexpected surprises of writing: first you strain your imagination to create a story, and then the story tells you what it's about.

Write and learn.

The Open Door

Sporting his usual pinstriped gray suit, white shirt and narrow, charcoal necktie, Leonard slowed his pace a notch as he walked by his secretary's desk, tightly gripping his briefcase. She noticed that he peeked at her, and was pleased she was wearing her new cream-colored blouse and turquoise pin. She didn't know that he wondered if her rust-colored ponytail, pinched today with a pale yellow ribbon, was a new hairdo and should be acknowledged as such, or whether she had simply been in a hurry.

"Good morning, Miss Hopkins," Leonard said, uncomfortable with the formality of last names, yet unable to break the ice.

"Good morning, Mr. Leopold," she said, with an equally formal response.

Jennifer Hopkins was relatively new at the office. She was stick-thin, and of indeterminate age — somewhere between 22 and 35. Leonard thought she might be anorexic. At other times, he imagined her as a budding cornstalk in early summer well before harvest. Her thinness was like a flag, reminding him of his fear of gaining weight.

Self-indulgence repelled him.

Breaking his usual routine, Leonard stopped in front of Jennifer's desk and smiled self-consciously. Surprised, she returned a half-smile before lowering her eyes, exposing a tinge of orange eye shadow.

"I need to prepare for the upcoming trial, Miss Hopkins. Please take my phone calls and give me any messages after lunch."

"Yes, sir. Hmmm…could I ask you a question?" she asked, recognizing a rare opportunity to say something more personal to him.

"What is it?" He glanced at his wristwatch.

"It's just…well…most people call me Jennifer…actually Jen, most of the time. Jennifer is good. Would you call me Jennifer?"

"Jennifer it is. Yes, sorry, I didn't mean to…I mean…that would be good…Jennifer. It's a pretty name. I like it."

He turned to walk to his office feeling somewhat disoriented.

"Thank you," she said.

Jennifer pulled the yellow ribbon of her ponytail closer to her head and tightened the bow. She picked up a pen, fiddled with it a moment and looked at Leonard, now facing the door to his office. She cleared her throat confirming her presence and sighed, feeling a strange pity for him, or was it for herself? He was her boss, but he wasn't really a boss, not like those of the other secretaries, who pretended familiarity, often too much so, in a teasing fashion that sometimes set off alarm bells. She loved that he respected her boundaries.

Leonard was different, she thought. He was a needy boss who made her feel as insecure as he seemed to be. Sometimes she didn't know which of them needed the other the most.

I haven't been attentive enough to her, Leonard thought, as he stood jiggling the loose doorknob until it caught. Why hadn't he just called her Jennifer? He knew her name. Well, he would now; he was sure of that.

He shoved the door closed with the heel of his foot as he entered his office, but it remained a crack open. He turned partway intending to close the door, hesitated, and went to his desk, leaving it slightly open. He could see Jennifer's feet through the crack of space from his chair when he leaned to his right, since the partition of her cubicle didn't reach the floor. He stared at the spiked heels – thin, like her – on her open-toed shoes. Her pink toenails were a shade lighter than the shoes.

"I'll close the door later," he mumbled, preferring to say it softly than simply think it, conflicted between concentrating on his work, as he typically did, and enjoying the pleasurable sense of connection to Miss Hopkins, now, finally, just Jennifer.

Shadows on the sunlit wall in front of Leonard's desk danced with random patterns formed by the bare twigs on the tree outside his window blown by the chilly winter wind. Depressing, he thought, cold. Always the same. Work, work, work – imprisoned by lonely ambition: summa cum laude from college; law partner seven years after law school; successful divorce lawyer. He was proud of all that, but really, what now?

What irony, he thought, being a divorce lawyer. Leonard the bachelor, intimidated by the opposite sex. Miss Hopkins! Ridiculous. She was as much Jennifer – Jen – as he was Leonard. Why didn't anyone call him Len? And what did he know of marriage or divorce? Nothing. Maybe that was better, he figured, since at least he harbored no biases. But neutral was boring. Who cares about a man who cares only for his own advancement?

His thoughts were interrupted by the sound of Jennifer's phone ringing in the outside office.

"Mr. Leonard Leopold's office; Jennifer Hopkins speaking."

"Oh, it's you." Her voice lowered.

Leonard leaned forward and strained to hear more.

"Bob, sorry....I wanted to call you back...yes, I know... sorry...no....maybe...gotta go...I'm at work you know...yes, I know...always...me too...gotta go...bye."

Bob?...me too what? What's going on? Bob? Leonard was intrigued. I bet he's tall. Jennifer is...what...five-one? two? I guess that's why she wears high heels.

Leonard was five-five, generously speaking. He sometimes joked that best presents come in small packages, but he stretched himself to look taller when he said that.

Leonard tried without success to concentrate on the upcoming divorce trial, but his mind kept returning to Bob. Jennifer's boyfriend? Were they living together? Her voice sounded strained when she talked to him.

The moving shadows on the wall faded as clouds drifted over the sun, casting a gray spell in his office. He looked at the stack of files on the desk and the scattered reminders to do menial tasks. Enough of this, he thought. I need a change.

When he went to the rest room Jennifer's desk was vacant, making the cubicle look sadly empty without her. When he returned to his office he closed the door and flirted with the idea of doing something radical. His fortieth birthday was in three days; if he didn't break his chains now, when would he ever take control of his life? What would Jennifer think if *his* office was empty and she didn't know where he'd gone?

Leonard worked until 7 pm. The next day he didn't appear at the office.

"He's probably running errands," Jennifer said to Jerry Thomas, a lawyer in the firm. "I'll let you know as soon as he gets in. No, Jerry, he didn't tell me he would be late today."

Ten o'clock turned into eleven, and lunchtime came and went. No Leonard. Jennifer took several phone calls, with messages from clients. One woman said, "Just tell him that his friend from the other night called."

A friend? Who's she, Jennifer asked herself. What happened "the other night?" Hmmm. Was private Leonard having a relationhip? Her heart sank for a moment, although this idea also excited her. It didn't seem like him though. Probably she's just a friend. But then again, she mused, if Leonard has a girlfriend, well, that's interesting.

Leonard didn't come to work and Jennifer went home at five o'clock, as always, feeling abandoned. She kept nibbling on her lower lip, a nervous habit. Should I call him at home, she wondered? Better not. He'll probably come in tomorrow.

Leonard didn't appear at work the next morning. At noon, Jennifer called his cell phone. Unexpectedly, she heard it ring in his office. Oh! Was he okay? She immediately used her key to his office to check. Leonard wasn't there, but his cell phone was on his desk.

"I can't imagine why he left his cell phone, no matter where he went," said Jerry, when Jennifer told him. "Well, he'll turn up, Jennifer. Weird guy."

Jerry was wrong; Leonard didn't turn up that day.

Against her better judgment, Jennifer drove by his house when she went home that night. Several newspapers still in their plastic wrappers remained by his front door. She wondered if he might be lying incapacitated, or dead, inside the house, but put that thought aside. Don't be silly, Jen. He's a healthy guy.

The next morning she checked in with Jerry again.

"He's still not here? Not a word. Sorry."

Then Jerry noticed Jennifer's swollen lip with spots of dried blood and her ashen face. "Did you notice anything unusual about him before he disappeared, Jennifer?"

"Not really."

"Nothing at all? Has he ever disappeared like this before?"

"Not since I've been here, but that's only been three months. He always lets me know if he goes anywhere. He's…he's… proper. You know, on time, correct. I could set my watch by his schedule."

"Has he ever mentioned family?"

"He's not married." She blushed. "I don't know anything about his family. I did drive by his place last night, just to check. The house was dark; newspapers were still by his door. I don't know…I hope he's alright."

"Anything else, Jennifer?"

"Actually, yes, now that I think about it. This may not be important, but he said good morning to me the day before he left, and left his office door a little bit open. He's never done that before. It was strange…well, I…I thought so anyway."

At 8:30 on the first morning of his absence, Leonard stood in line waiting for Macy's department store to open its doors for its before-spring sale. He was comfortable in a queue, where he was passive and anonymous, where he could eavesdrop and meld into the lives others. Finally, he had taken charge of his life!

He was on an excursion in his own town.

"Nicole," he heard in front of him, "I've been on the same trip, I don't know how many times – five, six? Do you know how much it cost me? Less than $500. Less! Why don't you hear me? No. Less! Stop the bullshit! I don't care. You just sat on your ass the whole time, doing your nails, ordering room service, tips galore. I can't believe it, Nicole: stop for god's sake! I did *not* tell you it was okay. What could I do? You just kept plowing ahead like some kind of train without brakes.

I'm not Rockefeller. I sell doughnuts to pay the rent. I've had it. That's it, Nicole. I'm through. Take those pink toenails and find yourself a banker."

The cell phone snapped shut. "Shit," the man muttered. "Fuck." He zipped his jacket and shifted his weight from foot to foot, as if that would warm him up. Steam flowed from his breath. "Damn. It's about time. Good riddance," he told no one in particular.

Suddenly the guy looked directly at Leonard and said, "Can you believe it? $2300 for a weekend at Rehoboth Beach! Who does Nicole think she is: Oprah? And who am I supposed to be: Donald Trump? Geez..."

Leonard nodded, thinking that he was glad that he wasn't in his twenties anymore. He shivered and looked at his watch. Another ten minutes until Macy's opened.

Leonard fantasized Nicole with short, dark hair, curly, and blue eyes with a mischievous twinkle. Jennifer's green round eyes flashed through his mind at the same time. I bet he calls Nicole back, he predicted to himself.

The cell phone of Nicole's boyfriend rang. Ahaaa, he thought. She's back. Leonard imagined Nicole saying, "Hi, Leonard. It's Nicole. I'm sorry. I'm lonely. Can you come see me?" Her sweet voice echoed in his mind, but Leonard actually heard, "Bill, we have a lousy connection. How the hell are you? I'm standing in line in front of Macy's to get a new sweater at today's sale. Nicole never gave mine back. I broke up with that bitch. Finally! Want to meet at Larry's bar tonight? Cool. How 'bout ten? That's when the action starts. See you later, man. Bye."

In the moment of silence after the telephone exchange, Leonard imagined Nicole's angry boyfriend and Bill that evening within a sea of young men and women all jockeying for sexual conquests. He always felt out of place in such situations. Who was he kidding? He'd never been in such situations. He just thought he would feel out of place.

A wave of loneliness swept over him. He wondered whether Jennifer might be older than she looked, maybe close to forty like him, but then figured that the opposite was probably true for very thin people like her, like him. Her red ponytail with its contrasting yellow ribbon flashed through his mind when the line started to move forward.

Once in Macy's Leonard wandered to the sweater department where he might hear a follow-up of the 'Nicole affair', but he couldn't find the man. Eventually he bought himself a gray V-neck sweater with black trim along the neckline, feeling frustrated that his medium size sweater cost the same as an extra large sweater although it had less wool. Life is unfair, he thought, as he paid the cashier.

Leonard ambled through the department store for some time and then went window-shopping along the main street. Although his law office was less than a twenty-minute car ride away, he had seldom taken the time to explore the area. It was like being in a new city. He grabbed a hamburger in a run-down diner for an early dinner. Determined to spend the next couple of days on the road, he booked a room in a nearby hotel.

In his hotel room, Leonard lay on the bed thinking of Nicole again, this time imagining her in a crew neck sweater that went down to her thighs. And then his thoughts switched to standing in line, going nowhere. He remained motionless, as if dead in a coffin, and dozed off watching the lid close, feeling claustrophobic. He awoke in the morning thinking of a woman with curly brown hair and blue eyes wearing only a man's crew neck sweater. She seemed familiar.

The new day was like an empty canvas, and he pondered what to do as he sat at the coffee shop. He ordered black coffee and a Danish. "No, forget the Danish," he added when he saw a very fat man walking down the sidewalk.

Leonard decided to go for a drive in the country that morning, nowhere in particular. He sped along with little traffic and felt delightfully free, until his mind returned to the upcoming trial. The thought was weighty, like the remains of a cremated body.

He noticed small birds flying in a jerky fashion between the branches that rushed past him as he drove. He imagined the birds panic-stricken, as if they didn't know which branch to land on. They didn't look as free as he felt when standing in line waiting for Macy's to open.

He turned on the radio and scanned stations for music. He preferred classical, but country was okay. It was jazz he detested, all that senseless improvisation. Suddenly Leonard saw a line of arrested cars in front of him and quickly applied the brakes. "Damn," he said aloud, but a satisfied feeling softened his annoyance. He would be in line again. He got out of his car to survey the situation and saw scattered groups of people standing by their cars.

"What's going on?" he asked the man next to him.

"I don't know. Must've been an accident. Better just relax. Nice day, eh?"

Indeed it was, with bright sun, a crisp forty degrees, and a few white cumulus clouds in an azure sky. He breathed deeply and feigned annoyance: "What rotten luck!! Hopefully it won't be too long," he said to the man, although he was pleased to have a destination: to get past the roadblock.

He went back into the car and heard a regional writer – Ernest Worthington – being interviewed. What a great name, he thought, both earnest and worthy. Is that really his name, or is it a pen name? He was drawn to the idea of two persons, the "real" and the "made."

"Mr. Worthington," asked the interviewer on the radio, "when did you know that you wanted to be a writer?"

"Oh, much too late in life. I was almost sixty years old."

"You served on an assembly line making Chevrolet cars for almost forty years, is that correct?"

"Yes sir, that's it. Stood in an assembly line and did my mechanical thing."

"It must have been boring," probed the interviewer.

"Oh, no. I loved it. I had my buddies in the line and knew exactly what I had to do. It was routine, not much pressure in that sense. And eventually you'd see the cars all new and shiny."

"I see. Writing must have been an enormous change for you," said the interviewer. "How did you make the transition?"

Ernest Worthington, Leonard said to himself. I wonder what he wrote.

"Yes and no. Not that much change and lots of change. I wrote what I heard in that line, so the only change was writing it down. And it was very different too. I wrote what I heard, but it only really felt like my life after I had written it. Funny, it was my life, yet it wasn't until I told people about it."

Leonard was in a trance. "Yes," he said, so quietly that it would have been inaudible if someone had been with him. But no one else was in the car, so it didn't matter.

"Could you tell our radio audience how you learned to write such a beautiful book with so little education in writing, Mr. Worthington?"

"Well, I really had no idea how to go about it, sir, but I knew I wanted to write. All the stories I heard working in that line for so many years, how Jim's little girl died of the pneumonia, and Sam's wife walked out on him 'cuz he didn't bring in enough cash for her tastes, and how pudgy Rick's twenty-third birthday present from his girlfriend was the first present he had ever received. That was quite something, getting a present for the first time when you're an adult. It was a clock radio. Rick cried when he told me about it, and tears came to my eyes also. I felt as if I had received the present.

"So how did I learn to become a writer, you want to know? I just took out all sorts of books from the library and copied my favorite passages, pages and pages of copying. It was automatic in a way, rewriting what others wrote, somewhat like working in an assembly line and listening to everyone else. I learned new, fancy words, and I got to know how writers put ideas together, and then I began to feel what they were telling, felt it in my hands from reading it and in my heart from copying, and I just went from there. I got my stories by standing in that assembly line listening to the lives of everyone else – eavesdropping – and then I learned to write them by copying what other people wrote and, by golly, I became a writer! Imagine that. Everyone else's stories became my book. It's not fair maybe, but that's what happened."

"Thank you, Mr. Worthington, for your time and insight. Remarkable. Congratulations on your book, *Absorbing Life from a Distance*, which I recommend to all of you out there listening. Next week we will be interviewing...."

Leonard turned off the radio and wrote down the book's title. He sat behind the steering wheel impressed with what he had heard. For the first time he could remember he wanted to talk, but he was alone.

The other drivers were in their cars now, and traffic started to move. He followed in line, and within ten minutes he passed a wrecked truck at the side of the road, with three policemen directing traffic to move along. He made a U-turn and headed back to his hotel.

"Everyone else's lives became my book. It's not fair, maybe, but that's what happened."

What's not fair about writing down other people's stories? he wondered. Isn't everyone a part of other peoples' lives?

Leonard went back to his hotel, had a quick dinner and went to sleep early.

His first thought on Friday morning was that he had to return to work Monday and make his final preparations for the trial. But it was his birthday today – 40 years old! He had a sense today would be special.

After brushing his teeth he weighed himself stark naked. The indicator edged over one hundred and thirty-five pounds. I must restrict my eating today, he thought, although he was also pleased that he had gained a pound while playing hooky from work. It gave him confidence that he was able to break the chains, and he indulged himself with a chocolate doughnut for breakfast. He then set off for a brisk walk feeling less anxious about his unstructured freedom than he had yesterday, although he did feel a bit guilty about not letting Jennifer know where he was. That made him anxious to get back, to see her again, if only at work. Maybe...

Leonard walked until he found himself at City Hall where he saw couples standing in line at the front door. Lines always popped up from nowhere in his life.

The weather had suddenly warmed, and people, anticipating spring, had shed their coats. Most of the women were nicely dressed. One was wearing a long white gown with a sparkling tiara on her hair; others had on colorful dresses, and a few were wearing blue jeans. The men, too, varied in their attire, but were mostly dressed up. A few wore jackets and ties, while others had sport shirts and sweaters. One grubby-looking, unshaved man, twenty-something, was wearing a soiled jacket, torn brown pants and a pair of gray running shoes. The sad-looking Hispanic woman with him, who looked four or five months pregnant, was impeccably adorned in a purple velvet skirt, a white lace blouse and shiny black, flat leather shoes. They made a strange couple, unsuited for each other.

"What going on?" Leonard asked the couple at the end of the line. A tall woman with a short man answered, "The Justice of the Peace is going to marry people for free today. It happens once a year."

Leonard joined the line just as it started moving. By the time he got to the front door eight couples stood behind him and more were on their way. Each person signed on a sheet of paper in the hall when they entered the building before they went into a large waiting room.

"By yourself?" asked the guard when Leonard passed the sign-up sheet.

"Yes…no, my fiancée is coming soon. She said she would meet me here. I better wait to sign the sheet until she arrives," he answered and then escaped through the door and took a seat in the waiting room. When he said the word "fiancée" Jennifer danced into his mind.

An eerie silence filled the room. Leonard felt awkward by himself. Many of the women fidgeted with their purses, or smoothed out their dresses, or just looked around. A few of the men seemed nervous and sighed occasionally. A teen-age couple whispered in the corner to each other, smiling and holding hands. They glowed like authentic gems surrounded by costume jewelry. Sweet kids, thought Leonard. I wonder if their parents know that they are getting married.

For the most part, the couples appeared thirty years old or younger, but several were much older, maybe even in the sixties or seventies. One balding man, fiftyish, was with a beautiful slim blond woman who couldn't have been over twenty-five. He kept kissing her on the cheek, while she inspected her shoes with downcast eyes. Leonard agreed that she had pretty sparkling shoes.

Leonard heard Ernest Worthington's voice invading his inner space repeatedly saying, "Everyone else's lives became my book."

"Please don't say that again," pleaded an obese man on the adjacent bench.

Leonard turned and saw the hard face and angry eyes of the woman sitting next to him. "Why not?" she said. "It's true, and you know it." Her fiancé stared straight ahead and his shoulders slumped.

Strange, thought Leonard. Are they really getting married?

And then Leonard heard a woman laugh across the room as she said, "I can't believe this." Her fiancé put his arm around her shoulders and squeezed, and she touched her right earring as if making sure it was still there. She moved a small inch closer to him, and Leonard drew his own arm closer to his body in response.

A side door opened and a jovial couple bounded out and left the room giggling. They were followed by the Justice of the Peace holding a sheet of paper from which he read "James Shannon and Deborah Rinse, please."

An enormous man with a graying mustache and shaved head stood up across the room and started walking proudly toward the Justice of the Peace. He wore a black shirt and immaculate blue jeans secured by a wide black leather belt with a turquoise buckle. He could have been a former Olympic gold medalist in the shot-put division and was so imposing that

Leonard felt insignificant being in the same room with this fellow. And then he noticed the feminine dot at the Olympian's side. The top of her head covered with tight black knots barely reached her fiancé's chest; from a distance she looked like his daughter. She had light brown skin and may have been African-American or Polynesian, or maybe she was just suntanned. Her eyes, polished onyx stones, were set in an expressionless, doll-like face. Her white dress shimmered next to her darkish skin. She wore no jewelry and needed none, so elegant a person was she, and so regal in demeanor that her massive fiancé blurred into the background once her tiny frame was spotted. She held a moist red rose in her left hand. She's so thin, thought Leonard, enthralled, even thinner than Jennifer, and so...so perfect. He watched Deborah Rinse take small steps alongside the pillar of a man about to be her husband.

Who would have guessed, said Leonard to himself, as he watched in awe as the two magnificent misfits followed the Justice of the Peace into his chambers.

Leonard had seen enough and did not want to tarnish this image with any other.

"I'm sorry, buddy. Maybe next time," said the guard outside the waiting room as Leonard walked past.

"Yes, thank you," responded Leonard. His voice bounced off the marble walls in the huge empty chamber – "yes thank you...yes thank you...yes thank you" – in a lonely, dying echo.

Leonard idled the rest of the day walking the streets and reading in his hotel room that evening.

Saturday morning he went home.

Jennifer was miserable that Leonard had deserted her without any explanation, but was relieved to some extent for the weekend. At least she would have her normal routine for the next two days. But the queasy feeling of abandonment remained and she felt almost homesick, like she remembered feeling when her parents had left her at camp when she was a little girl.

She was also worried sick about her boss.

She told Bob she was too tired and upset to go out that Saturday night. She had seen enough movies for a while, and that was all Bob ever wanted to do. After a quick breakfast Sunday morning of a slice of rye toast and a cup of black coffee she weighed herself, as usual: one hundred and one pounds. I shouldn't have eaten the toast, she thought. I'm over my hundred pound threshold.

She read and watched television the rest of the day and slept poorly that night.

Jennifer came to work early on Monday morning. She looked apprehensively at the closed door of Leonard's office, worried that he might not turn up.

Eight forty-five. Still early. She sat at her desk and began listing what she had to do. If he didn't come today, she would call the police and report him as a missing person.

"Good morning, Jennifer. How are you?"

Startled, Jennifer looked up and there he was standing before her: Mr. Leonard Leopold himself in his gray suit, pinstriped shirt and bland necktie, but sporting a new gray V-neck sweater.

"Mr. Leopold, my goodness, you surprised me!" she said, eyebrows raised and mouth agape. "Gosh, it's good to see you. I was so worried. Are you okay?" she asked.

"Yes, yes, fine," said Leonard, pleased with the warm reception.

"I …I don't want to pry, but where have you been? I didn't know you were going away. Gosh. Oh…that sounds so foolish," said Jennifer. She hesitated and took a sip of water. "You did go on a trip, didn't you? Just guessing, of course. I'm glad you're back. I…*we* missed you at the office and wondered where you were."

Jennifer sat upright, alert, eyes enormous. She swiped her hand over her hair, which was fluffy from the new shampoo she used that morning, and lacking a ponytail. She looked fresh and renewed. She beamed. She wanted to reach out and hug him. She sat stiffly in her chair. She felt thin and good. She absorbed his presence. She smiled. She took a deep breath. She waited.

"Yes, sorry. I'm fine. You're correct. I went on a short trip. I had some personal matters to take care of. I should have told you, or called…too much to do I guess. I didn't realize you were concerned." He suddenly felt important.

Lowering his voice, he asked, "You were really concerned?"

Jennifer wanted to tell him that she was worried sick, that she thought about him all the time, that she drove to his house looking for him, that things were not going well with Bob, that she bit her lip until it bled, that she didn't have breakfast this morning.

"Yes, I…Jerry and I were concerned." She wanted to tell him just how concerned she was.

"Is there anything new at the office that I should be aware of? Who called? I need to check my emails."

"Everything's fine here," she said. "Nothing important happened. Some woman called whom I had never talked to before. She said to tell you that your friend from the other night called. She didn't leave a message."

"Strange," he said. "Did she leave a number?"

"No."

"Thanks," is all he said. He looked perplexed.

"Why did you leave your cell phone here? Did you forget it?"

Leonard paused. "I guess I should have taken it. You were really concerned about me?" he asked again, looking at her red fingernails scraping the desktop.

"Yeah," she said. Relax, Jen, she ordered herself. She continued, "Is that a new sweater? It's really nice."

Careful, she thought.

"Thank you. I bought it at Macy's." He touched the apex of the V and added, "It was on sale."

"What happened to your lip? It's swollen?"

"Yes…no…I mean yes, I bit it by accident. Silly me. It's nothing," she answered. She touched it with the tip of her finger as if to both hide it and bring attention to it.

What *really* happened? Leonard wondered. Bob better not have hit her, he thought, getting angry.

Leonard noticed the small paper bag holding Jennifer's lunch in its usual nook.

"I…I wonder if…."

"Yes, what? If what?" she asked.

Leonard wiped his brow with the back of his hand and then scratched his head in a continuous motion. He saw in his peripheral vision two secretaries chatting and looking his way across the hallway. He glanced at Jennifer. He felt queasy.

"Just if…well…nothing really."

Then, from nowhere, Leonard asked, "Have you ever heard of Ernest Worthington? He's a writer. He wrote *Absorbing Life from a Distance*. It's supposed to be pretty good."

"No, never heard of him," she said.

In a rush of words, he added, "I heard him interviewed on the radio. Amazing guy, really, worked in a car assembly line his whole life and then he became a writer of other people's stories. I mean stories he heard from his friends in the assembly line."

Leonard switched weight from his left foot to his right. "Did you know that the Justice of the Peace marries people one day a year for free at City Hall, and that was last Friday?"

Jennifer looked confused. She wondered how he knew that. What he was trying to tell her?

Without waiting for Jennifer to answer, he continued, "I was there, by accident, that is. I saw this line and didn't know what was going on. I got in line...I was curious." He blushed. "I do that sometimes, get in lines."

"I didn't know any of that," she said.

"Yes...I must get to work now. Please take my phone calls until lunch."

"Sure, Mr. Leopold. Do you want me to order that book on Amazon?"

"Oh, that would be great. Would you please? Thank you... Jennifer."

He hesitated a moment and looked at the paper bag with her lunch.

"We could both read the book," he said, "and maybe talk about it at lunch after that."

Jennifer's eyes got just a little wider. "I love books, Mr. Leopold. Sure."

Leonard turned to his office and fiddled with the loose knob as usual. He left the door ajar. After inspecting the short pile of mail on his desk, he leaned to his right, and glanced past the door, more open than ever before. He saw Jennifer's red toenails poking through the open ends of her soft leather shoes, tan this time, with high, thin heels. He removed his jacket, loosened his tie and undid the top button of his shirt. He looked once more at the slim shoes on her tiny feet, and settled comfortably to work.

Immobilon

I am a jungle cat, perhaps a leopard but not quite, prowling on decaying leaves. The humid air has an organic stench with the sweetness of Rosalind's perfume. I sense tiny air movements, as if stirred by fairy wings.

Suddenly I'm Syd again, the accountant, slightly overweight, 47 years old, harried, in my study. Tax forms clutter the desktop. I hear angry clients shouting, "You're always busy, busy, busy, running here and there, but you get nothing done."

Time rewinds. My gray hair browns and covers my balding scalp. The creases in my forehead unfold. I'm in my twenties, standing in a pasture of dying grass, my arms limp by my side. I am paralyzed in mid-stride, my right foot leading the left. Rosalind stands before me in a white blouse, blue skirt and sandals, half-smiling, her soft curls and breasts close, yet so far away. Her turquoise-polished toenails shimmer like tiny lighthouses in the fog. She reaches out to me with both arms, beckoning. "Come," she says. "Why don't you come to me?" A man appears, takes her hand, and off they go, leaving me anchored to the ground.

She looks back, but he pulls her away from me.

Sunlight breaks through the window awakening me. I am paralyzed in the exact position of my dream, like yesterday, when Immobilon confined me to my study, wearing a T-shirt, torn jeans and bedroom slippers, without socks. My fingers can't grasp and my legs are like stone pillars. I can't move my head, but I can swivel my eyes. I can breathe with some effort. My senses remain sharp: I could feel a mosquito's sting, but couldn't brush away the insect. I can think, but I'm not sure whether that's a blessing.

"Oh, my god," I mutter. It's been two days. When will it end? Soon, I hope, but not really. I'm too young and scared to die. What have I accomplished with my precious life? Not enough. It seems I've run in place. I think of Rosalind.

Immobilon – the insidious gift from China that's sweeping the world. It strikes like a dart, paralyzing its hapless victims. Schools and public places have closed, but this hasn't slowed its deadly run. The virus - I'm assuming it's a virus - floats everywhere. Or perhaps it's some new virus-like thing liberated by all the genetic engineering scientists have done, or maybe even an invisible alien invasion from outer space. Dead and paralyzed bodies litter the streets and homes like mannequins. Adjacent victims speak to one another, although with difficulty, until the end. Breathing ceases in three or four days, sometimes five, less time than to starve to death. Some lucky ones won't catch Immobilon or will live through it, but not me, barring a miracle.

If Rosalind survives, I hope she remembers me.

Immobilon paralysis isn't painful, thank goodness. Strangely, it relaxes me, like a fine wine. Between bouts of panic, I feel grateful for this peace…how can I describe it?… this peace of letting go. Fuck those tax forms, fuck the phone calls I can't answer, fuck everything: Fuck! Fuck! Fuck!

Immobilon struck me like an iron club as I entered my study filled with Inuit sculptures I obsessively collect. How unexpected that these carved stones from distant lands I never saw made by artists I never met keep me company as life drains from me.

If I had another life to live, I'd give my love to living flesh rather than inert rock. Why didn't I "collect" Rosalind when I had the chance, before she married Ralph? My lifeless sculptures are no substitute for her. How tenderly she kissed my cheek when my rival was promoted in the firm instead of me, and how we cried together when we watched the veterinarian send her aging cocker spaniel to another world.

"You're my favorite," she told me more than once. And what did I do? I let her slip away.

"Stop!" I command myself.

I often wished I could ease the pace – slow down, hover – above the rushing flow of life, but I never did. Today, I want to move again, but am tethered to the ground. Immobilon has robbed me of a choice.

I see my neighbor Carl through the window in front of me. He is standing still as stone in his red checkered hunting jacket, captured by Immobilon with his right arm outstretched reaching for an invisible object. Snowflakes land softly on his shoulders, as they do on the fence post next to him. He must be cold. His open eyes suggest that he's still alive. Perhaps he sees me inside this room, and this makes me feel less alone.

Birds land on the wooden tray hanging from my windowsill that I always fill with seeds. Now they peck at barren wood. They will have to look elsewhere for winter food, poor souls. I've let them down. I've not seen a single immobile bird or other animal. They must be immune. Who said we humans rule the world?

I hear a knock on the front door. "Come in," I say, as loudly as I can. What luck that I did not lock the door when I came home two days ago.

I hear the door open, and then slam shut. Cold air whizzes past me, tinged with the sweet aroma of Rosalind's perfume. My spirit soars, but my body remains in place.

"Syd? Where are you?"

"In my study. Immobilon."

Her fragrance sharpens as she comes to me.

I think of the pasta and chocolate cake I have eaten at her house. A bachelor remembers things like that. I suspect *she* invited me, not her husband Ralph. He stared silently into space as we ate dinner. But, when the evenings closed, he shook my hand vigorously and would say, as if it were a script, "It was great to see you again. Good night." She, however, would touch my arm and smile, or sometimes hug me.

I never kissed her goodnight on the cheek as social protocol permits, because I desired it too much. Why did she intimidate me so, like when we drove to visit colleges together, or when we talked about our future plans and fears and…well, it goes on and on.

Rosalind enters my study. She gasps. Her pink lipstick glows in the light. I crave to envelope her tiny frame. She barely reaches my chin, yet I feel overpowered in her presence. Her essence fills the room.

Rosalind's gray-green eyes dart here and there, while mine are fixed on her since she remains in my line of sight. Her fingernails brush against my forearm, as if she's testing if I'm alive. Her touch gives me shivers, but she recoils.

"I'm so glad to see you," I say. "So glad."

Tears coat her eyes.

"It's okay. I mean, it's all right to cry."

How ironic! Pegged to die, I confort *her*, who is not infected, at least not yet.

"I'm sorry," she says. "Ralph's at home, immobile as the furniture, like you. I don't know what to do. I was hoping you could help me. Do you hear me, Syd?"

"Yes." I don't know what to say.

Rosalind sits next to me on the floor and rests her sweet head on my leg. The room darkens as the setting sun transforms the ice of day to evening ashes.

"Syd, I'm scared."

"Water, please," I say.

She looks grateful to be helpful. Why didn't I ever tell her that I needed her?

Rosalind returns from the kitchen and tries to get the water down my throat. Most of it spills on me. She throws the glass against the floor. I want to hold her. I try to will movement, to force it, but I can't. I try to calm myself.

When we were kids, Rosalind and I would see who could play dead the longest. I was always first to twitch or move a limb. She would laugh and say, "You just can't stay still; that's your problem, Syd."

Now it's not a game, and I can't move. I want to scream, but all I do is whisper, "Thank you. The water's good."

"I should go home to Ralph," she says. I sense there's a part of her that wants to stay.

"Really?" I say, meaning no, stay here; forget him. I'm dying too! For god's sake, tell her the truth for once. What do I have to lose? Ralph's a goner. She's here with me now, as in the past, when we were best friends in school together – sadly, only friends.

"Don't go," I plead. "You can't help Ralph. Look at Carl outside. Pathetic, isn't it? You can't help anyone beat Immobilon. But, you help me just being here. Ros...I love...I love you being with me...no...there's more...much more...I love *you*."

She blushes, hugs me, cries. "Syd," she says. "I'm so sorry."

I can't remember being so happy. And then I cry, without tears, unable to show how much I care on my frozen face.

"I'm so sorry," she says again. "For everything."

I'm sorry too, maybe even more than her.

She walks out the door and I am alone again with my sculptures in the lingering presence of her perfume. Night creeps in. I am fading into a thing in the distance. I feel drained of blood, yet, in spite of fear, I am curious of what is to come, as if some active force in me has been revived. I told her I love her. I said it! Oh, how great is that! I *love* her, yes, I love her, and now she knows. Maybe she always did. Maybe it's I who knows it now.

I hear a car passing in the street, and then a barking dog – lovely signs of life.

It's dark outside. I can't see Carl and wonder whether he'll freeze to death before Immobilon does its job. I feel myself falling asleep, like a horse, standing up.

I smell hay but it doesn't make me hungry. Rosalind comforts me. "Everything will be all right, don't worry, your paralysis is just a nightmare. I love you." I believe her.

I awake angry mixed with sadness. Everything will not be all right. Immobilon has not released its grip, and Rosalind is not here. I hate when dreams play tricks on me like that.

Blackness encloses me. I'm suffocating in a tiny space, like a casket. I try to break my panic, but I can't: Claustrophobia! "Help," I say for my ears only, since no one else is here. Rosalind's visit already seems so long ago. Her perfume still lingers. I wait for night to pass.

The morning sun retrieves my sculptures that keep me company. "Another sculpture?" Rosalind used to ask, grinning widely, each time I brought a new one home. "Are you making them your family – foreign brothers, sisters, cousins, what? Syd, good gracious, don't you have enough?"

"Enough? Nonsense. I love these guys," I always said.

How ironic that she was right, but in reverse. I'm joining *their* immobile family, not the other way around.

Rosalind never said so, but I know she liked my sculptures too. She would often pet one, or hold it and rub the patina with her thumb. I wonder whether I would've even bought them if not for her. I always asked myself, "Would Rosalind like that one?" If I thought 'yes', I bought the piece; if 'no', I passed it by. Each sculpture is part Rosalind, and infused in her.

I look outside again. The sunlight is bouncing off the snow. There's no wind, the bare branches are still, and a bird is perched upon Carl's shoulder. Who would guess we're in the midst of a silent devastation, and Immobilon, the enemy, is winning. I imagine that Carl is freezing, but…wait…I'm not sure. His eyes seem closed. Yes, they're closed! Oh, my god! Carl, a widower, my friend for many years, is gone forever. I wonder why he doesn't fall. Perhaps a gust of wind will bring him down. Death frightens me. How does one feel nothing? I wish Rosalind were here.

"Stop," I tell myself. Nothing hurts and that's a blessing. Settle down. Settle down? Get real! I think I have, for good.

The doorbell rings. "Come in!" I say, hoping it's Rosalind. No, she'd walk right in. The ringing stops. Another door unopened in my life. I'll never know who was there.

Rosalind flashes through my mind. I can't believe how obsessed I am with her. How is it possible I never accepted that before, when I could've acted? Why did I give her books and electronic gadgets on her birthday instead of the blue cashmere sweater that she liked but never bought, or perhaps the gold bracelet she said she could not afford? Why was I embarrassed to kiss her goodnight when we came home from movie dates, which due to me weren't dates at all? Why did I notice other women when I strolled with her?

"Is that muffled voices that I hear?" I ask myself, confused.

The voices fade as if they came from ghosts with no time or need to stop and say hello.

"What is that you said?"

"I said, 'Are those muffled voices that I hear.' Wait, who's there? Who said that?"

"I'm in front of you, as always, just where you put me. Don't be so worried. You are just like the rest of us sculptures, except, sorry, you're no work of art."

This voice sounds outside my body. I wonder how much I've mistaken in life as coming from without that came strictly from within myself?

"Since you can hear me, why don't you answer me?"

"Who are you? Where are you? I thought I was alone."

Actually, I *know* that I'm alone. This is very strange.

"Alone? How naïve! You're staring at me. Didn't you realize all these years that I saw you looking at me? You were too busy looking at yourself, I guess."

"Janus? Is that you?" That's impossible. Sculptures can't talk.

"Yours truly – a perfect name for what's happening."

"Why?"

"Don't you know? You named me Janus because of my two faces. But it's better than that. Janus was the ancient Roman god of beginnings, ends and transitions. One face looks ahead, the other one behind. It's the future and the past. That's your state, Syd. You're in transition, in the doorway."

Is this really happening? Am I talking to a sculpture? Am I still alive? Am I going crazy?

"Not crazy, Syd. Maybe now, finally, you'll see the truth. It's driven *me* crazy that you never recognized Rosalind's feelings for you, or understood your own for her. Too much moving, not enough sitting, I guess. Too bad for both of you."

I don't have any idea what's real or imagined anymore. Is this my entry into the netherworld? Am I going to start conversing with Carl? Let's see.

"Carl, how are you feeling, being dead, I mean?"

Well, that's better. I don't hear anything.

"Rosalind? You out there?"

Yes, it's still dead silent. I've definitely been imagining all this. Janus doesn't talk.

"Janus here. This is no mind game, Syd."

Now I know I'm talking to myself. I didn't say his name.

"You thought it, and that's enough. Language takes many forms for us works of art, and thinking is one of them, so careful what you think!"

Really? If that's true, the other sculptures should be hearing me think too. Is there anybody else out there hearing my thoughts now?

"I am," says a squeaky voice.

Good god! I've invaded my own privacy.

"Don't fret about such trivia," says another voice, much deeper and self-assured. "Privacy is an illusion, always has been. We're all part of someone else. Maybe I feel that way because I'm a piece of art that's bought and sold, traded, looked at, analyzed, judged, touched all the time. What's private?"

"Who are you?"

"Hey, I'm, Smiley, that funny looking musk ox made by Judas. You can't see me. I'm in the left corner of the room out of your sight. Whee-doodle-dah-dee and whoopee too. I'm so glad to be able to communicate with you now that you're becoming one of us. I've always liked you, although I *was* mad when you put me next to that wimpy bird for a while on the shelf behind you."

"What do you mean 'wimpy bird'? Some sculptures would kill to be on the same shelf with me."

Can't anyone get along, I wonder, even sculptures?

"We argue all the time and tell each other what we think," chipped in Janus. "Too bad we can't communicate with our human owners. It's a bit like slavery. They get so much wrong. Why do people always think they know best? Now that you're becoming one of us, you're privileged to learn the truth."

"Yes! Yes!" echoes the chorus throughout my study.

"You finally know what we're all about, Syd. All the pretentious talk of art critics saying that 'art speaks to them' were right, even though they never heard a word! How weird is that, saying the correct thing for the wrong reasons!" says Janus.

"Me, becoming one of you, a sculpture in my own collection? That's my transition?"

"Yup. You got that correct."

This sounds like science fiction. I don't feel like stone.

"Do you know what stone feels like, Syd? It's not sci-fi."

Can I trust a sculpture?

"Trust? I never told you to trust me, but I did think it. Wonderful! You can hear my thoughts now, just like I hear yours. The transformation is going faster than I thought."

"Tell me, Janus, if I become a sculpture, will I be immortal like you and the other sculptures?

"Sorry, Syd. I live strictly in the present. I don't have a clue about the future or legacy, and I don't care about the past. The past is the only death I know, so it's gone. And the future is always ambiguous. How could I guess who will buy me or break me, or whether I'll go to a museum, or someone's home, or get lost? Anyway, what's the difference? Do you think anyone really cares?"

I feel alone again. I want Rosalind to hear Janus. Do you hear that thought, Janus, or have you gone to sleep? Do you sleep?

Now he won't answer me!

I'll let the fog of sleep kidnap me.

A cozy, woolen blanket covers me. It changes from red to blue to green and then to…well, I can't say… I've never seen this color, but it's very, very beautiful. I am on a bed of feathers, or something else as soft. I'm in a solid space. It feels strange.

I see the sun and moon and stars, although they shed no light. It's neither night nor day. Snowflakes – white and black and purple – flutter downward from the sky and settle on the flagstone patio.

A movie screen appears. Charlie Chaplin waddles by, a funny-tragic figure. The scene changes, and Laurel scratches his tuft of hair, while Hardy has that silly grin. He waves his tie at me.

Hardy transforms to Albert Einstein doing push-ups and then he disappears. E=mc² flashes on the screen. A scattered, indifferent crowd applauds an empty stage.

Another scene change. Rosalind dances by herself. She is wearing a white chiffon dress, a diamond necklace and high-heel silver-colored shoes. My heart skips a beat or two. Mournful music flows from her. She looks sad. I want to dance with her, but she fades from view.

A train roars pass. I should be on it, but I'm not. I've missed the train.

A new voice wakes me up. "Don't be sad," he says. "I saw your dream. Transitions are always difficult, especially this one."

"Who are you?"

"I'm that small Inuit head just to the left of Janus, you know, the one that Rosalind always strokes gently when she walks by. I really, really like her! You can call me Tikky."

"After your carver, Tiktak?"

"Correct."

"You're right about the difficulty of transitions." I answer. "I miss Rosalind."

"Just wait. Immobilon may have tricks up her sleeve, so to speak. It's as Janus said, no one can predict the future. Remember how you used to dash in and out of here, always scribbling at your desk, always rushing to do something or other? So much movement; so many plans. Did that bring you Rosalind, or make even lesser dreams come true?"

He's right; oh god, he's right! I've missed the train all right.

I smell Rosalind's perfume. She's back!

"Hi," she says, almost as if relieved. "Are you ok? What a silly question! Sorry."

"I'm glad you're here, Ros. How's Ralph?"

She kisses my hand. I feel her lips, but can't respond, reminding me of how I lived.

"Ralph's dead." She squeezes my fingers and then hugs me.

"I'm sorry, Ros," I say, but don't mean it. "What will you do now?"

"Go on, if I don't get sick. Do I have a choice? Ralph had life insurance and I'll continue teaching school. I'm glad that he's not suffering. Oh! I'm sorry. How insensitive of me. I didn't mean that…I mean, I'm sorry, for everything, Syd."

I love it when she says my name.

"I heard on the news that there were very few new cases of Immobilon this week. People think the pandemic may have run its course. Dead bodies are being cremated. Trucks are collecting them in the streets and shops and everywhere. The government is urging to have the corpses burned immediately. It's like the Middle Ages. The cremators are picking up Ralph in a couple of hours. What a calamity!"

"Yes," I say. "I'm so glad you didn't get Immobilon. I hope you escape it. Please make sure that my body is collected when the time comes. I don't want to rot in here. Will you go to my cremation? I hope so; no one else I know will. I'm very, very weak. It won't be long."

"Of course. You mean so much to me. I'll never forget you."

I want to put my arm around her and hold her close.

"I know you'll think I'm nuts, Ros, but these sculptures have been talking to me. Can you believe it? They can talk and hear me, and even hear my thoughts. I didn't believe it at first when I heard their voices. I thought I was hallucinating, or perhaps talking to myself. But no, it seems I'm becoming one of them. Everything looks different. There's so much we don't know."

"Really?" she says, looking at me strangely. "What do you want done with all your sculptures?"

"I want you to have Janus and Tikky. They're special. Take them now so there's no confusion when I die."

"Janus? Tikky? What are you talking about? I thought you were paralyzed, not insane."

"Janus is the one with two faces. It's a long story. I know… but it's true. Tikky is the small Inuit head you often pat, the one with a scratch slanting slightly upward on the left side for a mouth. He's just to the left of Janus. You'll like them. Tikky has a crush on you! He's so lucky to have you forever. Be nice to them."

"Syd, I think you're losing it! Sorry, but it's true. Anyway, I'll take them home. You're right: I've always liked those two. Thanks."

"Will they talk to me too?" She asks, wearing her cynical grin that I've always loved.

"I'm not kidding, Ros, honestly. Someday you may hear them too. I don't know. They have their own little world, like we do. I've just had a chance to peek into theirs. I wish I never had that chance, but I did. I don't know anything anymore, except…" I'm suddenly at loss for words.

"Except what?"

"Except…I wish I had another chance with you."

"Oh, Syd. Me too. You've always been my special guy. I…I love you too. I'll never have another…"

She pauses and I wait.

"Another what?"

"Another…friend like you."

"Is that really it, Ros? Friend?"

"No, not really. I mean much more. Don't you know that? Remember when we played dead and you always twitched first? I wish we were playing that again. I want to see you twitch. I wouldn't laugh this time."

"I wish we could roller skate in the park again as we used to, and go to the movie tonight. I wouldn't even complain if you wanted to see one of those silly English comedies you always liked, and, damn it, Ros: I'd kiss you goodnight like you wouldn't believe. Even more. Why did I ever let you go?"

I surprised myself this time, but then I hear from her, "Why did I ever let you let me go?"

I'm speechless. I can't lift my hand to wipe my cheek, but I feel tears. She wipes my face with her hand. She leans her head against my shoulder. I'm not dead quite yet.

"Thanks for Janus and Tikky. I'll love them as much as I love you. And that's a lot. Does Tikky really have a crush on me?"

"He told me so."

She hugs me and I feel her body tight against mine. She kisses my lips and dries her tears.

"Good-bye, for now," she says, as if this were not good-bye forever. She leaves, cradling the two sculptures in her arms.

"Is anyone upset that I gave Janus and Tikky to Rosalind?" I ask the other sculptures. I hear quiet sobs.

"I understand," I mutter to myself.

And then I hear thoughts floating in the room that it's okay. I'm relieved, and tired, and then all goes black.

I wake up in Rosalind's living room overcome with her perfume.

"Yes, Mom. It'll be hard without Ralph, but, honestly, we never got along that well. We always fought and he was…I don't know…he wasn't Syd."

I can't believe my ears! She never got along with Ralph? He wasn't me? How did I get here?

"She brought you here after your cremation," says Janus, perched on the mantle.

"Oh, my god! How good to hear you, Janus."

"You know, Mom," says Rosalind, "before Syd died he was hallucinating that he was communicating with the sculptures. Poor guy. Immobilon must have affected his brain. But, what happened after the cremation is even stranger."

I'm cremated, and she went? I never felt a thing. What was so strange?

"Well, take a look in the mirror in front of you," says Tikky, who read my thoughts. "You look a little like me now, but not quite as handsome, in my opinion. I can still see your human features."

"Tikky! How wonderful to be with you again."

I look in the mirror but I don't see myself. No, wait. What's that head on the coffee table? I see a resemblance – my eyes and crooked nose. Good grief! I'm just a head, like Tikky.

"You got that right," says Janus.

"What do I mean, 'strange'?" continues Rosalind. "Well, they put Syd in the furnace to be cremated with a bunch of other bodies. There were so many dead people that they had to bunch up the corpses. It was ugly. It would've made you sick. The flames roared, friends and relatives cried, and I just sat there, thinking how happy Syd would be that I came to his cremation. He seemed to want it so badly."

Oh, yes, I am so very, very happy that you came, Ros. Thank you.

"Shhh," says Tikky. "Don't think so loud. I want to hear the rest."

"I know, Mom. Let me finish. After the flames stopped one woman asked if she could see the remains of her husband. The cremator told her there was nothing to see, but she insisted that she wanted to see his spirit in the ashes, so the cremator showed her inside the oven. I was curious to see too, so I went with them. When the door opened I noticed a head-like projection, like a baked ceramic piece in the ashes. It was soooo strange, but there it was when I looked again – a sculpted head!"

Good heavens, I thought. Was that my head?

"I couldn't believe it, Mom. I pointed out the head to the cremator and he said he never saw anything like it before. I asked him if I could take it home when it cooled down. He was confused, but said ok. It's just a head, he said, no body or arms or legs. And guess what? It looks sort of like Syd! It has his eyes and crooked nose. It's heavy, like solid stone. Weird. Syd told me he was speaking to the sculptures, and now this.

Anyway, I took the head and put it on the coffee table in the living room. As far as I'm concerned, it's Syd, sweet Syd. He makes me feel less lonely. I wish he knew."

Oh, I do, I do! She said 'sweet Syd'.

"Didn't I tell you to have patience? Things change." says Tikky.

"No, Mom. I'm not crazy. You'll have to come see it yourself."

Here comes Rosalind. She's looking at me! If only I could tell her that I see her too.

"Ros," I say. "Can you hear me?"

"Forget it, Syd," says Janus. "She doesn't hear a thing."

Rosalind caresses my head and moves me a few inches to the left. "That's better," she utters to herself. She also pats Tikky's head. I'm jealous, but how could she know that?

She turns away, puts on her coat and leaves the house. I'm left alone with Janus and Tikky.

She loves me, I tell myself. That's what I'll believe, and that's all that counts.

Little Boy Juan

"Juan, this is the third time today I've told you to stop talking and disrupting the class. How do you expect to learn anything if you're always yacking?" said his homeroom teacher, Miss Sprinkle. She couldn't help going a bit overboard in her language with him. He had to be punished.

Juan hated history class and so, once again, he was caught whispering to his friend Elroy, this time about his recent trip. He had accompanied his father, a scientist who was doing research on how animals protected themselves against freezing. The remote, treeless landscape, the ice water splashing his face in the zodiak, and the colorful houses – mostly reds and blues and greens – of the small communities looking like misplaced jewels fascinated him.

Katie in the front row also fascinated him, and when he wasn't babbling to Elroy he would stare at her with his huge black eyes. And her golden curls and freckled nose, well, perfect. He considered marrying her when he grew up. For now, however, he had to wait until Saturday, when his mother had arranged with Katie's parents that she accompany them to the park.

There was a problem though. His tough, unfair mother threatened to cancel the date if he continued getting in trouble with his teacher for talking in class. Maybe Miss Sprinkle would forget about this minor issue and then he wouldn't say another word. She wasn't that mean.

No such luck.

"Since it seems that you can't pay attention to the class, Juan, I must ask you to go sit by yourself in the empty classroom across the hall and think about keeping quiet until the hour is up."

With his head hanging low, like a dog with his tail between his legs, Juan dragged himself between the rows of students sitting obediently at their desks, his gaze fixed on the floor, amid snickers of his classmates. He felt humiliated by the holier-than-thou attitudes that his so-called friends were pretending not to have. Before he stepped out into the hallway, he glanced back at Katie, and she flashed her magic smile at him. Miss Sprinkle waited silently until Juan was out of the room and the door closed with its customary click.

Juan shuffled to the empty classroom, his prison for the next half hour, dragging the toes of his old sneakers against the floor. He heard Miss Sprinkle's faint, squeaky voice say to the class, "Sorry for the interruption. Now, who can tell me the name of the third President of the United States and what he is known for?"

Juan imagined Katie, her hand flapping in the air, begging to be chosen, as he thought "Adams...no...Madison? or was it Jefferson? Yeah, Jefferson. It's Jefferson." Katie would know that for sure. And then he pictured Thomas Jefferson, wig and all, on a sled driven by dogs across a barren snowfield. He couldn't remember what Jefferson was known for, but he was sure it wasn't dog sledding in the Arctic. He didn't care what Jefferson was known for.

Juan was a fragile, beautiful nine year-old boy with an aristocratic nose and pale lips. Despite tiny nostrils, he had an acute sense of smell, almost as if he was a dog, and he sniffed everything around him. The fresh, distinctive odor of snow in Baffin Island had been exhilarating. He continually brushed back a shock of his dark brown hair that fell loosely over his right eye with a quick, feminine motion, associated with a slight jerk of his head. He was the smallest student in his class, an inch shorter than Katie, but she didn't seem to care. His enormous, pathetic-looking dark eyes would make anyone want either to hug him or to cry.

The unoccupied desks with their attached swivel chairs made the prison-room seem even lonelier than it was. The musty smell of chalk dust reminded him of mold he had sniffed in the basement of his house once. "Homework assignment: Pages 110-128 of Chapter 12" written on the blackboard sent a chill through him. School was bad enough during the day; home was for playing. He was against homework in principle. He especially detested when his parents, mainly his mother, kept asking him if he'd finished his homework.

"Yes, Mom," he always said, whether or not it was true. Why did she care anyway?

Juan sighed heavily, worried that his mother would cancel Katie on Saturday. That would be terrible. Damn Miss Sprinkle!

Juan sat down at one of the chair-desks in the middle of the large room and looked around, trying to think about not talking, but this wasn't working because thinking was a form of talking, as far as he was concerned. The only difference between thinking and talking was that no one heard him thinking. He wasn't even sure that was true either. He often worried that others *did* hear him thinking because it was so loud in his head, like for example, when he was fantasizing about Katie, although she did have her annoying traits. Her "kissing up" to the teacher and her fake sweet smile did drive him crazy sometimes, and he let her know that in his thoughts in no uncertain terms, yet...he couldn't stop dreaming about her cute bangs and everything else. She had ice-blue eyes, nothing like his almost black ones. He wished she would, at least once, give the wrong answer in class, but she never made a mistake. He was convinced she was the smartest person in the world, even smarter than his parents or big sister, who was cool and smart, but not like Katie, who remembered everything she read or that the teacher ever said. Juan's friend Larry said Katie was a genius. But, what did he know anyway?

Genius or not, Katie was just right.

"Think about keeping quiet," kept echoing in Juan's mind, but he kept running into the problem that, as far as he was concerned, thinking was a type of talking, and that wasn't quiet. He tried to think so silently that no one would be able to hear it. That didn't work. Thinking was thinking. If he had to stop thinking altogether to learn new things in class, as Miss Sprinkle said, he would never learn anything.

"I'm just dumb," he told himself, but he didn't really believe it.

Clouds were gathering outside and the bright afternoon sunshine that streaked through the window and bounced off his desk disappeared. Without the glare, he saw scratches on the desktop, including an unfinished tic-tac-toe game that drew his attention. He filled in an X in one of the empty corners in his mind, but the game was unwinnable no matter what he did. He pretended he won anyway, and this made him feel a little better.

He suddenly imagined his mother glaring at him and saying, "Why can't you keep quiet in class? Now I've got to cancel Katie on Saturday."

The sun disappeared entirely behind a black cloud and the wind whistled outside. He shivered, remembering the freezing zodiac rides in the Arctic, although it wasn't cold in the classroom. He thought he smelled rain, but it wasn't raining yet. Why couldn't he trust his sense of smell anymore. But then again, if he smelled rain, he was sure that it would rain any minute. He trusted his nose.

The windowpanes looked filthy against the dark sky. Juan saw "Jimmy is a jerk" traced by someone's small finger that had displaced the dirt on the window. He remembered his father saying that a film negative is a "reverse picture" and that "the more transparent places on the film make darker images on the paper when it's printed." Remembering this made Juan think that the writing on the window was like a negative on a film, and he was proud that he figured that out himself. Then he wondered who the heck Jimmy was, but it didn't mater. He had never noticed before how dirty the windows were. But he had noticed that the windows either reflected images like a mirror or were virtually invisible, depending on how bright it was outside. Also, he had always been confused why a glass window reflected images right beside it. How did that work?

He didn't realize these were interesting questions.

He began to feel anxious, vaguely like he did when he woke up that morning from a nightmare that he was falling down a dark tube. It was awful.

No, that wasn't it. He was scared his mother would cancel Katie because he was talking in class.

Again, he imagined his mother saying, "When are you going to learn to keep quiet in class, Juan?" and then he heard his father say, "Yes, you really should make a greater effort to be good in class and do what your teacher says."

What Juan's father said never bothered him as much as what his mother said, because he knew his father was only trying to make his mother happy. His father only cared about his science stuff at work. His mother really meant it. He even felt sorry for his father sometimes because his mother would just yak on and on, especially at dinner. He wondered if his father ever wanted to send her out of the room to think about being quiet.

Juan tried to shut his parents out of his mind, so he tried to convince himself that he didn't care what they said. That worked for a little while, but not for long because he knew down deep that he *did* care what they said, especially what his mother said and thought, since she ruled the house and everyone knew it, even his sister Linda, who was fourteen. All these thoughts agitated him and he really, really wanted to be alone, so he got up and went to the back of the room.

His mother better not cancel Katie. *That* would make him furious.

When he sat in the back, everything seemed different. The room looked much bigger than it did when he was sitting in the middle of the room. He had to squint to read what was written on the blackboard at the other end of the room. He imagined the long line of empty desks in front of him filled with kids talking to each other, but ignoring him, as if he were an outsider, not really a part of the group, too small to fit in. Besides, none of them spoke Spanish like he did, and his English wasn't great yet. This made him anxious again, not really scared, but worried, and a little bit sad, like he often felt before going to a birthday party, or even before going to school everyday. He never could understand why he was always nervous before seeing other kids, even though he felt okay when he was actually with them, if they were being nice and not teasing him. His mother had told him that it was just the *idea* of being with other kids that was scary, and she said she loved him, but that wasn't helpful.

"It's amazing how big this room looks from back here," he muttered quietly to himself. His soft voice sounded strange when there was no one there to hear it. Then he tried to imagine what the room would look like if there were no walls. This made him think of the Arctic, where there really were no walls, and he wished he were there again.

Suddenly he smelled a strange, sweet odor that was kind of disgusting but good at the same time. He looked around to see what it might be, and he saw a half-eaten candy bar that someone had stepped on under his desk. He wondered whether one of the kids was eating it in class and threw it on the floor and put his foot on it when the teacher came by. That's what he would have done. Why else get rid of a perfectly good candy bar? He started feeling hungry.

He looked at the clock on the wall and saw it was 2:35. He couldn't believe that he had only been in the room for about ten minutes, because it felt like hours. He knew the clock wasn't broken, because the second hand was going around. He had another twenty-five minutes to go until the bell rang and the school day was over. Time just crawled sometimes, like now, and he wondered whether time always went at the same speed.

When he was in the zodiac looking at a couple of polar bears walking along the beach the time went so fast that it seemed like it didn't even exist. That was amazing!

He decided that he was definitely going to write a story about that. He hadn't made up his mind whether they would be talking polar bears, or even if they would be nice bears or fierce ones, but he would figure that out later.

It was as quiet in that big, lonely room as it was in the middle of nowhere in the Arctic. All that space and no cars or houses or anything, no noise of any kind at all, just space and more space, huge amounts of space with big rocks lying around everywhere. The thought of it made him begin to feel tiny, so tiny that he wondered whether he might disappear. In a way he liked that thought, disappearing, so when Miss Sprinkle came back to check on him he wouldn't be there, or anywhere else. Boy, would she be upset! But he had to be *somewhere*, everyone is somewhere, and he couldn't imagine where he would be if he really disappeared, so he forgot all about that idea.

Juan started ambling around the room, with no destination in particular. He had to stay in the room or he would get into even more trouble. And that would end Katie on Saturday once and for all. He dragged his hand along the desktops, one after another, and kicked the attached chairs gently now and then as he proceeded down the row of desks towards the head of the class, where the teacher's desk was. He stepped on a pencil, picked it up and stuck it in his pocket. What the heck, he thought. It's just a wooden pencil on the floor. It wasn't like he was stealing or anything like that.

When he got to the teacher's desk at the front of the room, he opened the center drawer and saw some chalk, a few thumbtacks and a piece of paper with a phone number on it. "Alice" was written next to the number. He wondered who Alice was, but soon forgot about that, took a piece of chalk and started drawing funny faces on the blackboard.

He was startled when he heard, "Hi, Juan. Feeling quiet yet?" at the door. He turned and saw Sammy run off down the hallway and go into the bathroom. A minute later Sammy bounded out of the bathroom and rushed back into his classroom without looking at him standing at the door. Juan suddenly felt very, very lonely, even more than before, and he wanted to pee but was scared to leave the room, so he sat down again at a nearby desk.

The sun peeked out from behind the clouds for a moment and shined directly in Juan's eyes, then disappeared again behind a black cloud, returning the room to a drab, unfriendly gray. Juan saw streaks of water flowing down the window. "I knew it smelled like rain," he said to himself, and this was comforting. He always loved rain for some reason. He didn't have to go outside at recess in the rain, and in Puerto Rico, where he lived until two years ago, they even closed the schools if it rained hard enough. He liked the idea of recess, but the reality was that he always stood around by himself while everyone else seemed to be having so much fun together. He didn't mind so much being alone, but it was embarrassing, like holding a sign saying "no one likes me."

Juan looked at the clock again: 2:47. "It wouldn't be too long," he thought, until his mother would pick him up. She was always on time. He could count on her being there with a snack for him. He wasn't mad at her anymore just then, but a wave of fatigue overcame him. He could hardly keep his eyes open, but he was worrying whether he should leave the room when the bell rang or wait for Miss Sprinkle to come and tell him he could go. Anyway, he didn't know what his homework assignment was and he needed to find out, as much as he hated homework. But, if he waited for Miss Sprinkle, who wouldn't get there until a few minutes after 3 at best, the other kids would see him banished in the classroom and laugh at him, and his mother wouldn't know where he was and be worried.

He always felt guilty if he was even a couple of minutes late and his mother would ask sharply, "Where were you? What were you doing?"

His eyelids became heavier and heavier and he didn't really want to make the decision as to whether he should wait for Miss Sprinkle to free him or just go himself when the bell rang, so he lay his tiny head on his crossed arms on the desk. It felt so good to let everything go for a couple of minutes. He couldn't remember when he felt so tired. The weight of his head on his thin arms comforted him, and he sighed deeply. His closed his eyes and the room became black. It didn't matter anymore if there were walls or if it was raining outside. Nothing mattered anymore. It was so peaceful, drifting alone in a sea of nothing in an empty room, being where he was supposed to be and not having to tell anyone anything, not even himself by thinking. He heard a bell sound very far away, as if it came from another planet, and he dreamed of kids milling around.

"Juan, wake up, wake up!" He felt his mother's hand shaking his shoulder.

"What? Where am I?" said Juan, startled and confused. He lifted his head and saw his mother and Miss Sprinkle through sleepy eyes.

"I've been looking all over for you. I was so scared! Finally, after all the kids were gone, I went to your classroom and, thank god, Miss Sprinkle was still there. She told me you were in this room, but she was sure you would have left when the bell rang ending the school day."

"Huh? Sorry. I didn't know…What time is it?"

"Time to go home, Juan," said Miss Sprinkle. "I gave your mother your homework assignment for tomorrow. I hope that you thought about not talking in class."

"Oh, yeah."

"Juan, when are you going to learn to behave in class? You've got to listen to your teacher if you're going to learn anything. What did you do sitting in that empty room for so long?" asked his mother.

"Nothing," said Juan, and then he yawned.

No word about Katie and Saturday, thank god.

Love Contraception

"Were humans on Earth anything like us?" asked Bettina.

"Not really," said her mother. "They were strange creatures who depended on appendages, legs I think they called them, to move from one place to another. Humans also had other discrete structures. Eyes, for example, for seeing, and ears for hearing. Once one has been integrated by harmonic oscillations with twitter, as we have, it's almost impossible to comprehend such crude, disjointed, structured creatures of the past.

"You will learn all this in school when you're a hundred years older. But you need to hear about *Starglow* and *Salawanda* now, as I did from my mother. You'll see. It's about love."

Bettina and her mother were cloudlets, which had evolved over eons of time for their beauty and efficiency on the tiny planet of Coddle. Bettina had reached the age in which she could proliferate and had that lovely violet lining surrounding her indicative of a capacity for love. She had started to fill the vacuum surrounding childspace, and gyrated whenever she mentioned Henle, a cloudlet roughly her age. That scared her mother. Love was the single remaining flaw from antiquity that threatened the equanimity of the planet that the RULERS fought so hard to maintain.

"Listen for once, Bettina. You need to know what I'm about to tell you."

"Okay. Go on, Mom."

"*Starglow* was a sweet, happy Thought, although complex."

"Am I complex?"

"Be still, let me continue. Yes, you are complex, like all adolescent cloudlets."

"What's *Starglow* got to do with me? I know all about Thoughts."

"Maybe so, Bettina, but I doubt you understand their origins and purpose. Thoughts broke free from the minds of humans on Earth and became independent entities that escaped to outer space, infecting other planets, including ours. That's when the trouble started, and when love became dangerous."

"Trouble? Dangerous?"

"Absolutely. *Starglow's* job, as that of all free-living Thoughts, on small, friendly Coddle was to inhabit Vibratons. The RULERS assigned the Thoughts to specific Vibratons. These assignments changed frequently then, as they do today, to maximize the enjoyment of Vibratons by increasing their diversity of Thoughts. Being a happy Thought, *Starglow* was expected to make Vibratons content and keep vibrating for a long time."

"Why was that so important, Mom, to vibrate?" Bettina asked, getting more interested.

"Well, the crucial role of Vibratons was and still is to maintain Brownian motion – constant vibrations producing heat. The sun is so much further from us than from any other planet that without the heat of vibration we'd reach absolute zero. That would be terrible. We would all freeze to death. If Vibratons stop vibrating, they become Statacoms – useless immobile structures – which are essentially death sentences for all of us."

"This sounds a little theatrical, Mom. Have you been inhaling spiked fog?"

"Of course not. Listen to me, Bettina, Miss Know-It-All. Wars didn't cause the extinction of humans on earth. It was boredom. Humans developed Statacom-like traits and they shriveled to nothing. Boredom kills in many ways, and here it's by freezing us to death. Do you want to become extinct? The RULERS need to use happy Thoughts like *Starglow* as public servants to keep Vibratons from boredom and transforming into the deadly Statacoms, which can't vibrate, if we're going to survive."

"Okay, mom. I get your drift. Keep going."

"Each human being had many thoughts in their gooey central control system called a brain, before the thoughts broke loose into free-living Thoughts."

"What's a brain?"

"Quit diverting me, Bettina. However, brains are important. Brains controlled everything for humans. That was a big problem. Imagine having each of your functions depend on just one centralized facility, a brain, that connected to every part of you with fragile, minute strands, nerves they were called, that could break or get sick and leave you impaired, or worse, dead. Obviously, a brain and nerves were a catastrophic mistake of evolution, and made life vulnerable, often even miserable, for these primitive creatures. And brains were terribly isolating too, because each clumsy brain was trapped in a single human. Brains made humans lonely."

"That's sad. It makes me want to involute."

"Oh, no, Bettina, that makes such a mess. Just listen and learn."

"Sorry."

"Brains, despite their defects, were able to generate many thoughts, which seemed at the time responsible for emotions.

Emotions created havoc and could be so destructive that some human beings did nothing but try to understand how thoughts and emotions were related, but they made little progress. It's all extremely complicated."

"What are emotions, Mom?"

"Good question, Bettina. I'm not sure how to explain it. It's so foreign to me. Anyway, humans didn't know yet that thoughts needed to dance to their own rhythms. Thoughts hadn't broken free yet. Consciousness was in its infancy. The result was that all the differing thoughts of a single human were as trapped within the individual as was the brain, which filled humans with conflicts, driven by emotions, that made them do self-destructive things."

"I can't even imagine it. I really do feel like involuting."

"Please don't!"

"Okay, okay. Maybe I'll just reverberate. Were thoughts anything like *Starglow* or other Thoughts that are assigned to Vibratons?"

"Exactly! You got it. One of evolution's big steps was to let thoughts escape brains and become independent. The Thoughts learned to multiply on their own. All this gets a bit messy, but the important point is simply this: humans had many thoughts trapped within their brains, all in a state of civil war, and then something happened in evolution that allowed the imprisoned thoughts to escape become our ancestral, independent Thoughts, like *Starglow*.

"Wow! That's pretty neat, but hard to believe."

"Nature is not simple, Bettina. In fact, release of thoughts led to an astounding discovery. Trapped thoughts in brains were assumed to cause emotions. But this turned out to be false. Emotions remained stranded in the humans even after the thoughts were gone. That's why humans scratched so much before extinction and were constantly oozing red stuff called blood. Envy, greed, ambition, jealousy, all things that would mean nothing to you, remained in humans after their thoughts were released."

"What's envy?"

"It was wanting something that another human had. It's not important, Bettina, it was a dead end path that no longer exists. But one emotion did get tangled in released Thoughts. I presume that it is on the way out, but it keeps emerging, even today, here on Coddle, and you have got to beware."

"What's that?"

"It's *love*. No one has ever been able to define it exactly."

Bettina's mother hesitated for a moment, sensing that her precise words were critical now.

"Let me put it this way, Bettina, it's a little like the uncertainty principle, which you studied in physics. If you describe the electromagnetic force attracting one cloudlet to another, it becomes impossible to recognize the tingling associated with love. However, the tingling also attracts two cloudlets together. If you focus on the tingling, the electromagnetic force can no longer be measured. You can't recognize both attractive forces at the same time. It's one or the other. And, here's the major problem, the tingling is love, which creates havoc."

"Have my orbitals ever fluctuated with love?"

"I don't think so, Bettina, thank goodness. But it could happen. And that's why you must remember the legend of *Starglow* and *Salamander*. You need to know about the importance of love contraception at your age."

"Love contraception! I'm all ears, mom. Ha, ha, ha, ha, ha. Ears! Weird. Go on."

"*Starglow* was almost full-grown, like you are now, and had been on several assignments for the RULERS. Since he was a happy Thought, every Vibraton he inhabited thrived. One of his Vibraton inhabitants actually increased the speed of Brownian motion during his occupancy and illuminated the surroundings with a rosey glow. Some say that was the origin of the name *Starglow*.

"Anyway, one day there was a Vibraton rebellion on a remote dustfield and Statacoms were beginning to accumulate. This had to be stopped quickly. If more than 30% of the Vibratons transformed into Statacoms, the area was forever lost. Thus, the RULERS sent their best Thoughts to this troublesome dustfield to quell the rebellion before it was too late, and *Starglow* was among the rescuers. When he got there Brownian motion was reduced, and the sheen was gone from many Vibratons. The RULERS assigned *Starglow* to one particularly small, sweet Vibraton. He slithered in through the snotchel between the thermolocutors, as usual. Some things never change.

"At first *Starglow* was all business. He went directly to the solemnichamber, poked around a bit to get a sense of what kind of delivery – monotonic, enthusiastic or somewhere in between – would be most effective for his particular Vibraton. In my opinion, if *Starglow* had a fault, it was his lack of spontaneity. But there was something special and different about this Vibraton that made *Starglow* tingle."

"Yikes! Tingle. That sounds dangerous."

"Right you are, Bettina. Just wait. *Starglow* didn't keep his cool and became impressed with the Vibraton's shiny rivets. And then, much to his own surprise, he broke the tradition of silence and said 'Hi there, I'm your new inhabitant. Glad to occupy you.'

"Also breaking tradition, the Vibraton replied, 'H-e-l-l-o.'

"Before *Starglow* had time to adjust to this unusual development, his molecules rearranged themselves involuntarily, to spell *SALAWANDA*.

'Is that your name?' *Starglow* asked.

'Y-e-s,' she answered, emitting a reddish color, and then she wiggled just enough to tickle him.

'Stop it!' he insisted.

'You're googly.' she said.

"*Starglow's* perimeter started flopping and his molecules began bumping into one another. Legend is that he serenaded *Salawanda*. He had no idea that the tingle he felt was love."

"Great word, *l-o-v-e*," muttered Bettina.

"*Salawanda* moved faster, glowed brighter and regurgitated compact lolleylanders more often than any other Vibraton in modern history when *Starglow* inhabited her. From the point of view of Brownian motion, *Starglow* was a great success. He found a way to mingle all his molecules with *Salawanda's*. They were both glowing. But, assignments were of short duration and, after what seemed like no time at all, a messenger arrived from the RULERS, who ordered *Starglow* to leave *Salawanda* immediately and go to Squarefield, where another special assignment awaited him."

"Oh, no, no. That's terrible," Bettina cried. "Tell me it isn't true? What did *Salawanda* do? What happened to *Starglow?*" Condensation dripped within her stratified layer, and she feared that she would certainly involute now.

"It is true, Bettina. No one had warned *Starglow*, or *Salawanda* for that matter, about love. Remember when I told you how dangerous love is, and how you must use love contraception to keep it as far away as possible?"

At that moment, Bettina's mother shivered as cold atmosphere flowed past her, and she understood that her relations with Bettina would never be the same again.

"So what happened?" Bettina asked, much more matter-of-factly than before.

"After the initial shock brought by the messenger, *Starglow's* molecules disconnected and he lost cohesiveness. Each of his molecules wiggled independently. He developed internal randomitis, and drooping sheets of sadness folded lifelessly around his perimeter, tugging at his core in all directions simultaneously, tearing apart any residual happiness he might have had.

"*Salawanda* lost her radiance and stopped vibrating. She never regurgitated another lolleylander, and her snotchel secreted a sticky substance barring any other Thought from entering. She was not even able to transform into a Statacom. She remained motionless, Thoughtless and empty as the space between orbitals for all eternity. She was a new form of dead. "

"Poor *Salawanda*," whispered Bettina.

"Yes, indeed: poor *Salawanda*, and poor *Starglow* too," said her mother.

"*Starglow* oozed away from little *Salawanda*, as devoid of energy as she was filled with the ambient cold. He stretched slowly in one direction, then another, and reoriented his molecules to try and imagine what his new assignment would be like, but to no avail. He traveled less than twenty kitopters from *Salawanda* before he froze and became transparent, indistinguishable from the hard, grey rock supporting him. He was never seen again.

"*Starglow* and *Salawanda* had tasted love, the old fashioned kind from human antiquity, and there was no returning. It's emotions, Bettina; oh, the danger of it all," said Bettina's mother, as her voice dropped a decibel or two.

After a moment of silence, as if in mourning, with all attention directed inwardly, Bettina's mother looked up and found herself alone. Bettina was gone, with only a puddle of icy condensation left in her place. When Bettina's mother gazed towards the horizon, she recognized that familiar violet glow emanating from her daughter's fuzzy cloud. She also saw a bouncy little cloudlet floating next to her that was clearly Henle. He too seemed to glow, but with a softer, bluer light. Their edges ebbed and flowed, overlapping and entangling each other, becoming one and then separating again, over and over, without apparent concern, as they drifted out of sight.

Bettina's mother shrunk her perimeter and contracted her core. Her stratifications bloated. "I tried," she uttered softly, and then she closed her padoodles.

Compression

Rodney Stik, a meticulous man of twenty-two, picked up the black and white photograph of Deloris and kissed her cheek as he did every morning. This particular morning he said, "See you in a few hours," since he was going to fly from his home in Washington, D.C. to Los Angeles to meet her. But not everything goes as planned, as you shall see. It is unlikely that you will believe what happened, but as you chew upon the facts I doubt you will be able to come up with a better explanation. Also, I was Deloris's college roommate and know that she was impeccably honest. She swore me to secrecy until she died. Sadly, that happened last year, so now I'm free to relate the story.

The story begins with Rodney, the most inflexible person in every way I ever knew. It's necessary to know that in order to believe (if you can) what happened later. He was tight as a drum. Stretching for him was a nightmare. When he exercised with Deloris, he watched in awe as her muscles elongated and contracted effortlessly, over and over again. Trying to touch his toes, whether sitting on the floor with legs extended or standing, even with bent knees, was impossible. Rodney just didn't bend. Period. As an aside, Deloris loved to exercise with him. I think it made her feel like a natural athlete. She was a bit of tease, however. She used to wear progressively tighter

T-shirts each time they exercised to keep his attention. I must say it worked.

Rodney met Deloris in the library at American University in Washington, D.C. while cramming compulsively for a mid-term exam in engineering. She was browsing leisurely through a fashion magazine, and he envied her, what shall I call it, her nonchalance. He also liked that she was much shorter than he was, that she sneezed with gusto, while he suppressed noisy sneezes by pressing his finger against his upper lip, and that she didn't bother to whisper when she spoke to him in the library. After they dated a few weeks, he discovered that they differed in many other ways as well: she was oblivious to details, generally late, loved surprises and hated routine. She lived in vivid colors; he in shades of gray.

"If only…," he thought many times. "If only I could be more like her."

Rodney was obsessed with Deloris. She literally danced in his mind constantly, but then he worried that he didn't know how to dance, or that he would step on her toes if he tried and make a fool of himself. He daydreamed that he played hooky with her, just hanging out, or going for a drive, but then he fretted that his professors would notice his absence, or that he would not be prepared for class the next day. As he lay in bed at night he imagined her singing a lullaby to him, which made him feel peaceful, but then he wondered exactly where she might be at that moment, or whom *she* might be thinking of, or singing a lullaby to. Was it him? When Deloris beamed her radiant smile and touched him on the arm in a way that made him feel important, a nagging inner voice told him that she might be doing that also to other men. And he worried some more. Poor Rodney. He was so uptight that he was utterly unable to roll with the punches, to absorb the shocks in life, to be squeezed and rebound.

Rodney really liked Deloris. It was less obvious that *she* liked him, but she did, a lot. Opposites attract; it was as simple as that. They dated in college and became a steady item. She loved his blue eyes that glowed light blue in the sunlight, more aquamarine than their deep sky-blue sheen in candlelight. (That will turn out to be important later; keep it in mind.) She appreciated his dry, self-deprecating black humor. "You should live in a black box, Roddie," she'd say when he complained about this or that, "then you would shine by comparison." But she loved that he needed her to be happy, and she saw his incessant self-doubts as endearing qualities, genuine modesty, refreshingly different from other boys who were always showing off. Although his constrained, rigid personality could be exasperating, it allowed her spirit to roam within safe borders. Being with Rodney was...comfortable.

One week after graduation Rodney and Deloris were having dinner in a Chinese restaurant during a fierce thunderstorm. Suddenly during the meal, Rodney crossed his fingers, took a deep breath, and looked at Deloris with intensity.

"What is it? Is something bothering you?" she asked.

"Err, Deloris, I wonder...that is...would you...well..."

She fidgeted and straightened her chopsticks on the plate.

"You wonder what? Would I what?" she asked.

"Well, I really like you...I mean...I think...no, not think...I..."

"Whoa, that thunder is LOUD!" exclaimed Deloris.

"Yeah, I'll say. Deloris...I...I love you."

There, he thought, I said it. And then he worried that he didn't convey how much he meant it, and that made him anxious that he was worrying about that. If she was going to be his wife explanations shouldn't be necessary.

"I know, Rodney," she said, blushing. "I love you too."

"Will you...marry me?" he asked.

She accepted. Just like that. Imagine. What a woman! I was dumbfounded when she told me, but that was Deloris through and through. Unpredictable. Lovely. Impulsive. Accepting. I loved her myself.

Whether or not Rodney would have suffered the same fate if she had refused his proposal or if he had become engaged to someone more like himself will never be known. It is not a trivial question. There's scarcely a person who has not wondered from time to time what life would have been like if they had travelled a different path.

They decided to wait before marrying. Rodney wanted to be gainfully employed before taking on the responsibility of a wife or starting a family. Deloris agreed and got a job in the gift shop of the National Gallery of Art on weekdays and volunteered as a docent on weekends.

Meanwhile, poor Rodney struggled. He had many job interviews with different engineering firms, but his attempts at self-promotion were clumsy. He tried without success to impress his interviewers with his strongly held views, such as his love of perfectly proportioned buildings and distaste of asymmetric structures designed by avant-garde architects. He was unable to soften his strict opinions on any topic – the best way to build hydroelectric plants, the dangers of nuclear power, the importance of covenants to make housing developments completely uniform. He had unflappable views on everything. His interviews always ended with, "Thank you, Mr. Stik, we'll call you." He was grateful that while in college he had saved enough money from summer jobs as a carpenter's assistant to subsist during this difficult time. After six months, he became irritable and depressed.

"Rodney, I need a break," Deloris said one day. "I think it would be good for both of us if we separated for awhile."

Rodney blanched. "Really? What are you planning to do?"

"Don't worry," she said. "You'll be able to concentrate on finding a job and I've always wanted to see the West Coast. I thought I'd drive from Seattle to San Diego and explore the little towns along the way. As soon as you get a job I'll move back and we'll get married."

"Do you still love me?" he asked, looking vomit-green.

"Oh, Rodney, yes. Don't ever doubt that. I do. This will be good for both of us. You'll see. Nobody gets a job immediately. You're doing great, and this gives me a chance to do something I've always wanted to. We're so lucky."

She was adamant in her gracious style. He had never known this firm and practical side of her, and he admired the magical way she had of turning adversity into opportunity.

Just as electromagnetic attraction between plus and minus weakens with increasing distance, Rodney missed Deloris. But it's safe to conclude that he was also relieved to have some freedom, although even the idea of freedom was threatening. A few days after she left, his imaginary walls began to recede and he felt his space enlarging.

One Sunday morning when he was skimming the classified section in *the Washington Post*, his eye caught sight of an intriguing job advertisement. A Mr. William Short was searching for a long-term employee in his fledgling retail business. He had just opened a store called "Dimensions" that sold measuring devices. Several pieces of merchandise were listed to describe the store. A ruler labeled in reverse for southpaws caught the attention of left-handed Rodney. Another intriguing device was a specialized instrument that used infrared beams for determining the distance between two objects. The job appealed to Rodney's appreciation of precision.

When Rodney called to apply for the job the next day, Mr. Short said, "Great. Can you come now for an interview?"

Rodney was unaccustomed to such a positive response and went immediately with an uncharacteristic bounce to his step. Stiff at first, he relaxed a bit when Mr. Short said, "Call me Bill."

"Thank you, Mr. Short...I mean...Bill." It was difficult for him to remove the constraints of formality until he knew someone very well.

Their meeting flowed like water on greased glass. Rodney was drawn to Bill's obsession for precision. After the obligatory exchange of information, they started betting on the number of paces it would take each of them to walk across the shop wall to wall considering the lengths of their respective legs. Although 6 feet, 4 inches tall, Rodney took maddeningly small mechanical steps to cross the room and then apologized for being so rigid in his manner of walking; Bill, who was 6 feet, 6 inches and proud of being the tallest Short in his family, needed fewer paces to cover the ground. Rodney told Bill about Deloris and mentioned that she was only 5 feet tall.

"Really," said Bill. "That's short."

Rodney accepted William's offer to start working that day. At his first attempts at being a salesman that afternoon, Rodney was frustrated that the customers cared more about design of the devices than their precision or reliability. He then tried unsuccessfully to convince a customer that measuring was an exciting, adventurous journey, but received only a yawn in return. By the end of the afternoon Rodney decided to not say anything and let customers decide for themselves what they wanted, with the result that he sold a $500 attachment for a microscope to measure minuscule spaces. That made him indescribably happy.

Rodney delayed telling Deloris about Dimensions. He was superstitious that if he were too enthusiastic too soon, his good luck would disappear. More to the point, he worried that Deloris wouldn't approve of his becoming a salesman instead of an engineer. But Rodney felt dishonest withholding from her and was uncomfortable trespassing into what he considered a dangerous double life, which would be an unacceptable violation of his personal rules.

Rodney finally called Deloris after a week. His enthusiasm escaped his protective shield, much to his own surprise. "Deloris, I'm so excited. I'm working everyday, a great job, I love it," he bubbled, unaware that he'd forgotten to ask about her. Deloris was hurt to be ignored, but overcome by his ebullience, a side of him that she had never seen before.

"What engineering firm are you working for?"

"I'm working for…Dimensions… but…it's…not *exactly* an engineering firm."

"What is…Dimensions, you say?" Deloris sounded confused.

"It's…it's a store for measuring things."

"A store? You're a salesman?"

"Well, yes, you could say so. But you should meet Bill Short. He's the owner and really smart and nice and I'm making money and it's really, really a good job, with a future I think. Bill loves to measure things, like I do, and he talked about a lasting partnership. He wants me to work with him, not just for him."

As Rodney rattled on about his rapport with Bill and how much he liked his new job, Deloris understood that he was not going to be a practicing engineer, at least not now. The more she heard the more she began to see the benefits; frustration changed to acceptance.

"Now we can get married, Deloris," he said while she was absorbing all this new information.

Deloris was a practical woman, as I told you earlier. Rodney was right; now they could marry, as she'd promised to do once he found employment.

Rodney said he would visit her in Los Angeles the following week and they could plan their wedding. He made airline reservations that evening. There was a special rate available between rows 15 and 30 in a new aircraft that flew a bit faster than the older model. Four extra rows had been squeezed into the plane allowing the airline to collect twenty-four additional fares. Rodney was pleased to save $57 and spend 42 minutes less in the air than the usual 5 hours and 36 minutes. He didn't consider the loss of space he would suffer.

So far the story is not unusual: Two young college students fell in love, had differences that they believed could be overcome, and planned to get married. No one has difficulty believing this; it's garden-variety stuff. What came next if what challenges belief. However, it explains Deloris' mysterious acquisition of enormous wealth. But, I'm getting ahead of myself.

Rodney arrived at the airport more than three hours before departure time, catering to his compulsion to be early. It turned out that the plane was delayed by almost two hours before boarding and then remained on the runway for an additional two hours because of a faulty valve in the decompression system that had to be fixed. When the plane did take off, Rodney must have been in a foul mood and quite agitated, although how he felt at that time can only be inferred.

Deloris went to the airport in her favorite blue dress to pick up her fiancé and proceeded to the gate, as this was before the security rules prevented people from meeting passengers at the arrival gate. She watched the passengers leave the plane when it arrived, but no Rodney. She waited another five minutes and when he didn't appear, she called his apartment and then his cell phone. She got voice mail both times. Confused and anxious, she called Bill Short at Dimensions.

"Hello, Mr. Short, this is Deloris, Rodney's fiancée. I'm at the airport to pick up Rodney, but am really confused. His plane just landed, but he didn't come off with the other passengers. He doesn't answer his home or cell phone. Do you know what's going on? Do you know if he came to Los Angeles today?"

"Hi, Deloris. Rodney's told me all about you and was excited to see you again. He wasn't on the plane? Strange. I've no idea where he is."

"Was he okay yesterday, I mean, feeling well, or worried about anything? You know how Rodney can be sometimes."

Bill said that Rodney was at work the previous day. He was nervous and kept munching on donuts and potato chips all afternoon, but otherwise he seemed all right. He also told Deloris that Rodney got angry with a man who couldn't decide between two brands of lasers for measuring distances and lost the sale.

"That's not like Rodney," said Bill. "When I got upset that he had been rude to the customer, Rodney said that the guy's a jerk and – please excuse my French, Deloris – but… Rodney said that the guy should go fuck himself. Sorry. That's not at all like him. Actually, Rodney was right, the guy was a jerk, but… well…you know…gotta to be nice to customers. I don't know what else to tell you. I wish I did."

Deloris thanked him and sneaked on the plane when the attendant looked the other way. Perhaps he was sick and still on the plane. There were lots of newspapers, soiled napkins, pillows and the like strewn about that the flight attendants were cleaning up, but she didn't see Rodney. She asked an attendant if there had been a tall, thin, blue-eyed, twenty-two year-old passenger on the flight. Deloris explained that he was her fiancé, she had come to pick him up, but he didn't come off the plane.

"Oh," Deloris added, "he's very uptight."

"Uptight. Yes, I know exactly who you mean," said the attendant. She told Deloris that a man fitting his profile had sat in seat 19A. He had rung for her repeatedly for all sorts of things: water, information, such as how high the plane was flying, how much longer until they arrived, and so on.

"He was very nice, polite but…high maintenance I would say," said the attendant.

Deloris nodded knowingly.

"He had such bright blue eyes," added the attendant.

Deloris went to seat 19A, a window seat. She was surprised at how close the rows were to one another in this section of the plane and wondered where Rodney would have put his long legs. She also thought it odd he'd accepted a window seat. He'd told her that being trapped in a window seat was like being stuffed into a sardine can with the lid sealed. But what came next was so astounding that it needs to be described in detail. Bear with me.

Deloris saw a crumbled shirt jammed in the corner of the seat similar in color to the upholstery, a pair of faded jeans lying on the floor, and socks and jogging shoes under the seat in front of Rodney's. Confused, Deloris removed the wallet from the back pocket of the jeans and saw Rodney's driver's license. She picked up the shirt and was startled when a large, glittering stone fell from it. She leaned down to pick it up but was distracted by a ballpoint pen under the seat next to an airline vomit bag with funny handwriting on it partially covered by the jeans.

"What's going on here?" she muttered under her breath.

Using the pen she scribbled on a napkin lying on the armrest. The color of the ink matched that of the writing on the vomit bag. She next picked up the bag gently between her right index finger and thumb, as if she was holding something sacred. The writing looked chaotic, with lines slanting up and down, and sometimes the letters looked like they were jumping off the page. She imagined a musical score for an irregular drumbeat that might accompany a relentless march to who knows where. She scrutinized this mysterious bag trying to make sense of it and read the first line.

"How could've I forgotten my diary? DAMN!"

This question jarred her. Strange, she thought. She knew of Rodney's obsession about writing in his diary. She continued reading.

> *I cannot chase the image from my mind of relaxed strangers lounging comfortably in first class, skimming the newspaper or appearing absorbed in their own microcosm, completely separated from us lemmings streaming to our appointed slots in tourist class as we boarded this god — forsaken flying tube, this pencil stuffed with carbon in the form of human flesh. The thought of their half-filled glasses of orange juice fails to moisten my dry mouth as I sit waiting for the stewardess, pretty but vacant, certainly no Deloris, who I'm supposed to marry, to bring me a glass of water. I guess she forgot: too many other people to contend with, too little significance in my thirst. If only I could pee, or take off my sweater. The first seems impossible since it would mean overcoming the nearly perfect living barricade of sleeping passengers on my left; the second is totally out of the question. I am already in considerable pain from having tried that stunt over Chicago. My back muscles are still in spasm from trying to maneuver my right arm in the few inches between the back of the reclined seat in front of me, my body, and the window to my right.*

Is it 4 inches between my forehead and the head of the gentleman in front of me? Maybe 5, certainly not 6. Anyway, I should decide whether I want to pee or drink. It seems ridiculous to do both. Maybe drinking is better since sweating may take care of my peeing needs. God, it's not just water I need. I need A I R. There's no air in here. Wait. Relax. I can breathe. See. In out, in out. Yes, but still…I need air. The vent above me seems broken. I can't unscrew it anymore and I don't feel any fresh air. I'll close my eyes. That's better. I'm in a desert. No, that thought makes me even hotter. I'm in the arctic, brrrr, beautiful white snow all around me. How I always wanted to go to the arctic: igloos, caribou, translucent icicles and glistening diamonds in the frozen snow fields. Space, s p a c e, s p a c e and condensing vapor from my mouth, visible proof of my existence. No, it's not working. I still can't breathe. Anyway, I can't keep my eyes shut; they're on springs; keep popping open. I'll look outside – that's s p a c e for you. The clouds are so far below; nothing above. Where does it end?

Deloris felt light headed as she read these anguished, desperate words. And the way marriage was mentioned, as if it were a punishment, left a pit in her stomach. She collapsed on seat 19C on the aisle and stared at nothing. The flight attendant came down the aisle and noticed the jeans on the floor.

"What's that?" she asked, and then was appalled when she looked at Deloris. "Good heavens! Are you all right? You look devastated, as if you've seen a ghost or something awful."

"Yes…no…I don't know. Maybe I have. The jeans…yes. What do you think?" said Deloris. "I'm sorry. I'm not sure what's going on. Please leave me alone for a few minutes."

The perplexed attendant, who still had much cleaning up to do, reluctantly left Deloris trying to compose herself. Deloris struggled to figure out what all this meant. She quickly gave up the idea of checking out the lavatories to see if he was there since it was obviously impossible for him to leave his clothes at the seat and walk naked down the aisle. In fact, this ridiculous thought made her want to laugh, which made her feel guilty. She pinched herself to make sure she wasn't having a nightmare.

She turned the vomit bag over, took a deep breath and started to read the other side.

> *Thank God for the nice man next to me, a bit weird but he does take my mind away from its self-imposed misery. He has a funny name I couldn't quit e understand. Something like Mumbo-Jumbo. What's the difference? He's a bit gruff, kinda FAT, about 44 inches around the waist I'd guess, and has big feet, real big. They Smell a bit too. He got all excited when I told him about "Dimensions". Told me about James Bradley. Never heard of him before. Measured exact angles from the earth to stars, accurate to six decimal points. Imagine that, and in the 1700s too. By measuring changes in these angles over a year he proved that the earth moves around the sun. Showed Copernicus was right. Changed the way people thought about themselves, about Heaven and earth, changed just about everything. And all the guy did was measure angles more carefully than anyone else. Never discovered anything solid. Angles, empty space, nothingness; nothing you could bite into. It had more impact than real things. Imagine that. I always knew that measurements were*

critical. Precision, accuracy. Can't beat it. Oops, the guy in front of me just put his seat back. HELP! I'm getting squeezed., feel the roof of the plane beginning to crunch me. Funny type of crunching, it's from my insides too. There, shifted in my seat a little. Gives me an extra inch or two. Jesus it's crowded in here. No A I R, none, feels like I'm surrounded by nitrogen. Stop it, Rodney. You're losing it. Get back to reality. No more writing nonsense. Ouch, my back. Water. Air. Old fatso next to me is sure snoring loudly. Wish I could get his damned arm off my leg. Shit. Air. Deloris, I need you, how muchlonger? Another2hoursat least. I need you.

When Deloris read her name and that he needed her she dropped the bag on her lap and her eyes moistened. She wished she'd been there too. How Rodney was suffering. She retrieved the bag and read the last few, compressed lines. She could hardly make out what he was saying.

I wonderif weareontime. Stewardesss, arewe on-time? HeyallIsee is fatso's armon myleg. Where'smy leg?Icansee theseatwheremyleg used tobe. Mylegistransparent! Ohmhgod! Icantbelieveit, my armtoo. Icanseerightthroughit. helpI'msoscaredsomethingisterriblywrongstewardessI'mturningintoglass. Where'smywater?, airhelp. Icanstillfeelmyleg, but it'sgetting smaller. Idon'tseemtohave any fingersonmyhand. Everythingis transparent, disappearing. HeyIseemtohavemorespaceIdon'tneedairsomuch anymore IsthatglitterIseesomingfrommyarm?It'speaceful, like-cozy, likethewomb, more compressed: delorisdelorishel-logood-byegood-byeImissyouIloveyouhaveahappylife

*what'shappening?I'mgoing,goingdisappearingstill-
herebut can'tbeseencan'tbeheardcruchcrunchmole-
culesgettingtighterandtighterandit'soverhelpme,no
don't,it'snotsobadgood-byelivingworldgood-bye,goo*

Nothing more was written. Deloris sat, drained, clutching the bag. After a moment, she picked up the shiny stone on the floor, cuddled it tenderly, and began to cry.

"What happened?" she asked herself.

Deloris sat, miserable and baffled, as the attendants finished cleaning up. She tried to make sense of what she saw. "Is it possible?" she wondered, half aloud. "Could Rodney have actually been *compressed* into this rock?"

Slowly, as preposterous as it seemed, she began to believe that uncompromising Rodney had, in fact, been squeezed to such an extent that he'd crystallized to diamond.

She had many questions. Had the airline crossed the threshold of packaging people safely? Was he too rigid to survive such compaction, especially in a window seat with no aisle to relieve him? Could he really have been so stiff, so unyielding, that he became a catastrophic victim of economy class and company profit? If that were so, Deloris imagined that the bluish emanations of the diamond came from his beautiful blue eyes now locked in his crystal structure, and her heart melted.

Deloris put Rodney, his wallet and the vomit bag in her purse and slipped out of the plane before the attendant had a chance to question her. She went to the baggage claim to check whether she could find his suitcase. She asked a very fat man that fit the description on the vomit bag if he'd sat in seat 19B next to Rodney.

"Yes, M'am, sure did," said the fat man.

"The man sitting next to you in the window seat was my fiancé, but I can't find him. Do you have any idea where he might have gone?"

"No, Ma'am. He's a nice guy, but a bit uptight, I'd say, kept complaining that his bones bones were crunching. What a sense of humor!"

"Yes, I know. But where is he?" asked Deloris.

"I have no idea, M'am. I fell asleep and the attendant – nice woman – woke me up after we had landed. Everyone was off the plane already so I got my stuff together and here I am. He must have gotten off too, but I don't see him. Sorry I can't be more helpful. Oh, excuse me. There's my suitcase."

Deloris waited until all the baggage from the flight had been collected. One familiar looking suitcase remained un-claimed, and it had "Stik" and Rodney's address on the iden-tification tag. Although she believed, as incredible as the idea was, that she knew what happened to Rodney, she took the suitcase to the airport security police and thought it necessary to report him as a missing person. She didn't mention the stone, the vomit bag, or the wallet. She knew they wouldn't have believed anything she said.

Still dazed in disbelief, Deloris went home presuming that Rodney was in her purse. She put him in a clear Plexiglas box with a wooden handle carved in the shape of a rose and placed him on her bedside table next to his photograph. She kissed him before going to sleep every night as she looked at his pic-ture, and said good morning to him every day when she woke up. Sometimes she took him to the movies with her. She talked at him about many topics, including politics, architecture and, especially, gossip. From time to time she asked him with appre-hension exactly what he meant when he'd written on the vomit bag that he was *supposed* to get married, and then followed it with questions concerning his anxiety about the need for space. Well, she thought, was he more satisfied with the space he had now? She also got angry when she imagined he refused to stray from his rigid views, or when she thought he disagreed with her, but overall this was rare. Usually she believed that their opinions were similar, especially as the weeks went by. She often laughed out loud when she pretended he told her a funny, absurd story that he embellished with outrageous, politically incorrect or obscene remarks. When this happened she was amazed and amused to think that these off-color yarns were coming from Rodney, whom she knew from the past to be maddeningly straight. All this she kept absolutely to herself.

As Deloris's imagination transformed Rodney into a creature of her making, it became increasingly difficult to free herself from him. He sparkled now in his new form instead of being dull as before he crystallized. It had become her turn to be obsessed with him instead of the other way around. But despite her infatuation, she was a practical woman. Rodney was an inaccessible man, now partly her own creation, and she had to let him go. She also rationalized that this would be kindest for him, for she imagined, or hoped, how frustrated he must be to lie by her side every night in his transparent box, with nothing to do but watch her, even though that thought excited her.

The police called a few months after she had reported him as a missing person and said that they'd explored every avenue and had no explanation for his disappearance. The airline attendant had, of course, found the clothes at seat 19A, but there was no wallet or other identification. Rodney's absence was listed as an unsolved mystery, probably a criminal act of some kind that led to his demise. His parents, friends and Bill Short had no choice but to accept Rodney's presumed tragic fate.

One year later, Deloris realized his potential value as a diamond, and she took decisive action to start a fresh life. She had Rodney appraised.

"It's the biggest, most symmetrical and perfect diamond I ever saw!" said the jeweler. "I've never seen the likes of it. It's worth at least five million dollars, maybe more. Where did you ever get such a diamond?"

"Oh, it's a long story," she answered. For some reason, the jeweler, a good-looking man about her age, inspired trust and she needed to tell her story to someone, so she did.

"That's ridiculous," the jeweler said. "Never mind. What I don't know won't hurt me. I certainly can't afford to buy it and I doubt that any of my clients could. But let me give you some advice: Put that rock in a safe place!"

She assured him she would, and pleaded with him to never tell anyone about Rodney's transformation. He looked at her disbelievingly, but agreed that her story would remain strictly between them.

Deloris took Rodney to the Getty museum to see if they were interested in buying him as a jewelry display for their section on rare gems. They were overwhelmed with the size and beauty of the diamond. The experts from the museum peered into the gigantic, clear stone with sophisticated instruments that Rodney would have loved. They concluded he was a flawless diamond with the most beautiful blue, almost aquamarine, glow they'd ever seen. The Getty paid eight million dollars for the diamond, making Deloris into a rich, single woman.

Although selling Rodney restored her freedom, she missed him a great deal. She kept his Plexiglas home by her bedside for some time after he was gone, although seeing the empty box made her sad so she eventually put it in a drawer.

The jeweler who had initially appraised Rodney, an Italian named Secondo, read about the record sale in the newspaper and called Deloris to congratulate her. One thing led to another and not long afterwards Secondo proposed, presenting her with a small emerald engagement ring. He thought, understandably, that a diamond ring would be inappropriate. Deloris accepted his proposal with the same ease that she'd agreed to marry Rodney. They named their first son, who by chance had bright blue eyes, Rodney. Within five years they had another son and a daughter. Although I'd been Deloris' best friend since our sorority days together in college, it wasn't until after the birth of her daughter that she finally told me the whole story. To the best of my knowledge, Secondo and I were the only people she ever confided in. Now many years have elapsed and Deloris has passed away, and so has Secondo, so I feel free to tell her story. In any case, here's how it ended: she never really got over him.

After her marriage, Deloris continued to go secretly to the Getty museum to visit unfortunate, compressed Rodney. When no one was looking or in hearing range, she whispered to him about her life and feelings. She never told anyone else but me about these rendezvous', not even Secondo, whom she grew to love very much. She would gaze for hours into Rodney's magic universe and imagined him say in his quiet monotone, "Please enter my world of eternal order... I'm waiting for you...no hurry...I'm not going anywhere." She hypnotized herself by repeating these words over and over; she became his queen and he her king, and they roamed happily together in parallel lives in his crystal paradise.

Empty Pages

The city of Florence slept at midnight in the gray-black humidity of a hot July. Gentel Pinskal, still jet-lagged from his trip from Ohio the day before, strolled the dead-empty streets feeling lonely and foreign. The deluge of science dissolved in the mist. He hadn't come to this conference on gene expression for information anyway; that was available in the scientific journals. He was escaping abandonment.

"I need a life outside of test tubes, and Annie needs more attention that you're giving her," Rachel had told him a year ago. Gentel retreated to his laboratory, angry that she didn't understand the pressure on him to achieve tenure. After the divorce, he became a tenured Associate Professor, but now his success felt empty. Rachel had moved to San Francisco and in the process had stolen their daughter, Annie, sixteen, with an asymmetric smile so captivating that even her crooked teeth looked adorable. He talked to Annie from time to time on the telephone, but with each call she sounded increasingly detached. "I'm fine, Dad," she'd told him before he went to Florence, but he became worried by the way she mentioned in passing her new boyfriend.

"What's he like, Annie."

"He's really nice, Dad."

"What else? Tell me something about him."

"Well, he's got a heavy gold chain necklace, an amazing snake tattoo on his right arm, and a pony tail. He wants to make movies."

Gentel realized the Rachel had been right: Annie was more important than tenure.

Despite the late hour, woozy from the many glasses of Chianti chasing the mugs of dark draft beer, and the long day of scientific talks, Gentel continued exploring the neighborhood. The only sounds of life in the deserted streets were his footsteps and the muted motor of an occasional car or motorcycle in the distance. He was drawn into a narrow alley by a dim glow from a lamp that sprayed orange-yellow in the air.

Squinting, he saw an archway ahead with a stylish lady's shoe with a very high heel protruding from a stone pillar framing the archway. He heard muffled, feminine sounds as he edged closer to peek around the column.

A youngish man with a half-open shirt and tight pants held up a woman whose knees were bent and her arms limp by her side. A gold crucifix with a thick gold chain dangled against the man's chest. Annie's boyfriend flashed through his mind. A ring with a stone on the man's finger pressed against the woman's face.

"*Holy shit,*" thought Gentel, scared to be seen.

The woman was thin, frail appearing, and only about five feet, Annie's height when he last saw her a year ago. But the victim before him was no child, and her abductor was no parent. Her short hair was in disarray, the color hard to discern in the pale light. Her sleeveless, blood-drenched blouse was ripped, exposing her left breast. Blood seeped from a gash in her side and formed a small puddle with short streams between cobblestones. His hand covered her mouth, suppressing weak groans.

Gentel tiptoed closer to the maudlin scene: a young assailant gripping a young woman, not much older than Annie, in an alley at midnight in medieval Florence. Jesus nailed to the cross hanging from the man's neck reflected soft light from the incandescent lamp and contrasted with the shiny steel blade of the knife that the man held. The curved blade, stained with blood, tapered to a needle-sharp point. The wood handle had a dark patina and a silver plate that capped the end.

Suddenly the two men locked eyes. Gentel froze, his eyes wide. The attacker grimaced and lifted the knife, threatening Gentel. He shook his head slowly from side to side as if switching roles from criminal to policeman.

Disoriented, Gentel imagined the assailant saying, "*Look at what we've done!*" The abductor dropped the knife and vanished into the dark, just like that, like Rachel, like Annie, leaving Gentel alone with the woman. She folded to the ground like a torn silk scarf. He leaned down, touched her arm and brushed the back of his hand along her cheek. She felt clammy and remained stone still.

"What an angel," he muttered. "What a perfect, human angel."

A fleeting image of Annie stabbed to death gave him a chilling pang of guilt, for letting Rachel take his little girl away, for being neglectful, for not being able to help the young woman lying at his feet.

He sat on the curb, stunned, confused, feeling inadequate.

"*I have to do something,*" he thought, suppressing panic.

In her early twenties at most, the lady wore a thin wedding band on her left ring finger. He slid his arm under her head, lifting it from the hard cobblestones, and placed her shoulders tenderly on his lap, as he had done so often not to awaken Annie when she'd fallen asleep.

Suddenly, her eyes opened to narrow slits and her right thumb twitched.

"Are you alive?"

Silence. Her eyes closed again.

He placed his ear against her chest listening for a heartbeat, but heard nothing. He searched for a pulse from the jugular artery on her neck, but detected nothing. He put his cheek next to her mouth; no breath. He squeezed her fingers and pinched her firm cheek. No sign of life, but how could he be sure? He wasn't a doctor.

"Help! Can anyone hear me?" he yelled. No response. He tried again. "Is anyone around, anywhere?" He heard a faint whirr of a motor scooter fade away in the distance.

And then his panic increased when he repeated to himself the accusation he imagined hearing: "*Look at what we've done!*"

Desperate to regain his composure, he gazed at the cobblestone street with the scraps of trash strewn here and there, the closed shops, and took a deep breath. He then looked at her, lying peacefully, her lips parted just enough to show a glint of white enamel behind her coral lipstick; her eyes were closed, beyond sleep. Her head and shoulders nestled on his lap, naturally, comfortably. Her soft hair smelled of fresh pear. Surely she's gone now, he thought.

He picked up the knife and was startled to see faint initials – AP – inscribed in the center of the silver plate at the end of the handle. *"Annie Pinskal!"* He wiped the blood off the blade with his fingers, and then dropped the knife in horror when he realized what he was doing.

"Perhaps AP stands for the manufacturer," he thought, or the initials of its owner.

"I'm so sorry, so very sorry," he whispered, looking at her peaceful body.

He leaned against the pillar, his grey shirt stained with her blood. He embraced her waist, partially covering the mean slash on her side with his hand, strangely cherishing this moment in the alley. The blood from the wound was drying.

The assailant's angry, accusing eyes flashed through his mind.

"*I didn't cause this, did I? She was stabbed before I came, wasn't she?*" he asked himself, but his cruel inner voice tortured him. "*You let him get away. You heard a scooter in the streets. There might have been someone to help. But you wanted to be alone with her.*"

Gentel caressed her body with his eyes, her weight soothing against his thighs. He started to talk to her as if she were alive, as if she would understand his feelings, which Rachel never did and which Annie couldn't because she was too young. He closed his eyes and spilled his heart. It didn't matter that she couldn't hear his words. Feeling her perfect little body press against his was all that mattered. Her blood on his hand felt warm and right, perhaps partly because it was so wrong, so illicit, yet exciting.

They became one in a dream world between life and death.

"Science is…well…I need more," he told her, "I want love." The word love reverberated in his mind, "…*love…love…love.*"

His mind drifted momentarily to the biography of Michelangelo that he'd read about recently, and wondered how much was true and how much imagined by the author.

"I've always wanted to be a writer," he told her, "to create my own paper world. I'd like to write a poem about us running away together to another country where they speak a language neither of us knows, and…"

Abruptly, he stopped talking as panic invaded his fantasy again.

"What am I doing? Am I nuts?"

He gazed at her high cheekbones, delicate brown lashes, lightly applied greenish-blue eye shadow, and tiny dimple that he noticed for the first time marking her chin: he'd fallen in love with perfection, with a woman who was married and dead.

How could he explain this situation if someone strayed by now? He had to leave the scene immediately. Before escaping he covered her breast with her torn blouse and placed her head softly on the ground. "Sleep in peace," he said.

He didn't think to rub off his fingerprints from the handle of the knife next to her before he left. He'd never been trained in crime.

Gentel slept until noon the next day. Imagine; he could sleep! He was that drained. Later that afternoon he told his colleagues that he had a bout of diarrhea, too much dinner he presumed, and apologized for missing their lectures. He thought about reporting that he saw a dead body in the alley late the night before, but it was too late, the police would want to know why he didn't go to them immediately, and then he remembered his fingerprints on the knife handle. He didn't think anyone saw him in the area last night, but how could he be sure? What if someone *had* seen him? He had to act as if nothing had happened.

He scanned newspapers and watched the news on TV the next two days before returning home, but there was no mention of the murder. This confused him, but he thought it must have been reported in some local media. He couldn't suppress dreams of the sweet pear odor of her hair and the light pressure of her body against him when he flew back to his barren apartment in Ohio.

Her image consumed him for the following year.

Gentel returned to Florence the next summer as a member of an international advisory panel for funding his field of research in Europe. After his first day of work, he went back to the alley where the murder had occurred. The narrow street felt empty without her presence. He wondered who had found her. He sat on the curb where he had the summer before and imagined her on his lap, but his arms wrapped around himself now instead of her waist.

"I'm so sorry, so very sorry," he said again quietly, as he had the night he'd discovered her. During his moments of recollection and mourning and guilt, tourists and residents walked by, glancing at him sitting on the curb as if nothing unusual had ever occurred there.

When Gentel's panel discussion concluded the next day, he went to the library archives of newspapers in English searching for homicides a year ago in Florence. He checked lists of deceased persons in the small print of obituaries, hoping there might be some clue identifying her, perhaps mention of a knife gash on her left side or with luck a small picture. He visualized her face as clearly after a year as if it were yesterday. He found no trace of her.

Gentel returned to his colorless, bachelor existence in Ohio. He dated on occasion, mostly blind dates from friends, but he thought only of her. "I'm sorry, but I'm not ready yet," was his standard line when the dating evenings ended.

He focused on his research, watched television, and obsessed about her. She became the phantom woman he shared his life with, much as a child's imaginary friend. He spoke to her in muted tones. That he didn't know her name kept her mysterious, a woman of his dreams, a clandestine, invisible mistress, with none of Rachel's imperfections and reproaches. It was as if her previous life had been preparation for her secret affair within him. She seemed happy enough in his mind, smiling and laughing at his jokes, and he loved that. He imagined that he felt her move sensuously on his lap rather than lie motionless as she did the night of the murder.

She was completely his now.

Gentel's intimate, imaginary relationship with her intensified his sense of guilt. He agonized about not having tried hard enough to save her, and worried that someone had seen him there that night, perhaps from a nearby window, or had noticed him leaving the scene, and eventually would accuse him of murdering her. Or, ironically, perhaps the man with the knife had told the police that he saw him stab her and had sketched a picture of him. His story would be corroborated with Gentel's fingerprints on the handle of the knife. It was just a matter of time, he thought. But there was no news of her murder, as if it had never happened.

Every time someone knocked on his door or the telephone rang, Gentel worried that it was a policeman who might say, "*Excuse me, but did anything unusual happen when you were in Florence for a scientific meeting in July, 1972? We have some questions about a brutal murder of a young lady and have reasons to think that you might know something about it.*" Gentel listed all those "reasons" in his mind many times.

Although tormented, he also had a nagging sense that if she *had* been alive and if he *had* saved her, she would be in Italy with her husband rather than with him. This gave him a tinge of satisfaction that he did not save her. Would he act the same way again? He didn't know, and concluded that it was an irrelevant question. Circumstances never repeated themselves exactly.

Gentel's imaginary relationship distracted him from his career, which faltered disappointingly. He published little and gave lackluster lectures to the students. He suffered recurrent nightmares. One was of handcuffs bearing his initials, G.P., and of people staring at him as if he was a murderer. Another was of her looking at him adoringly, but always fading into the distance.

A third dream was more detailed. It started with him conversing on a park bench with a strange man, while she watches nearby. The stranger tells him that he's just back from Florence, where he was studying criminology. Gentel asks him if there were many murders in Florence. The man answers, "A few, mostly crimes of passion. It's painful when a young woman is the victim." *When a young woman is the victim…a young woman the victim…*echoes in Gentel's mind as he sleeps. He sees his love reaching out to him, her blouse torn and covered in blood. She disappears in a narrow tunnel lined with cobblestones. The scene changes and Gentel is perched alone on a hard, wooden stool in a cramped, windowless dungeon. A bright beam of light coming from nowhere glares in his eyes. He asks a uniformed policeman with an enormous badge bearing the initials A.P. with the same font as was on the plate on the knife handle if there are many unsolved murders in Florence. The policeman retorts, "You seem very interested in murders. Did something happen to someone you know in Florence?" Every time at exactly this point in the nightmare, Gentel woke up, drenched and anxious.

These dreams continued for twenty years.

In his mid-sixties, Gentel decided to put his life in order. He left the university and rented an apartment in Florence, uncertain whether he was running away from his life in Ohio or bringing her home to her native land.

Soon after he arrived in Florence he returned to the cobblestone street and sat in the same spot where he'd fallen in love. He heard her say, "*Thank you,*" in his mind as he sensed her soul return gratefully home. He now felt like a widower. He decided to stay in Florence.

One day he wandered into a store with enticing leather-covered books displayed in the window. When he entered he saw many other similar books lined on shelves and stacked on tables.

"Can I help you?" asked the shop owner with a captivating smile. Gentel took an immediate liking to him.

"Yes, please. You have such beautiful books."

"Ah, thank you. Pick one up. Feel it in your hands."

Gentel opened a small book with gold embossing on the leather cover. The book was filled with empty pages of hand made paper. It was magnificent. He looked through several more books.

"These are wonderful!" Gentel exclaimed, running his fingers along the bindings. "They're pieces of art."

"Si," answered the shop owner, immodestly. "Thank you. I, Giorgio Bellini, made each one."

Gentel looked around the shop, picking up books at random, appreciating the high quality of the leather covers, and marveling at the impeccable taste of their designs.

After some small talk, Giorgio, who also took a liking to Gentel, showed him a nook in the back of the store where he was restoring ancient manuscripts. He carefully turned the pages of a seventeenth century tome that he was restoring, speaking Italian so quickly that the only thing Gentel understood was that he was in the presence of an artist.

They returned to the main part of the shop and Giorgio picked up a book and hugged it. "The empty pages. Hopeful, no? They're about emotions not yet expressed."

The scene was surrealistic: a man lost in his own creations in a land of empty pages waiting to be filled. Each book offered a new life to anyone with the courage or imagination to step into it, to write his own story.

Gentel scrutinized the books. The compact ones fit neatly in the palm of his hand; each one was a jewel. The larger ones begged for a pen to inscribe stories of love and yearning on their blank pages, to breathe life into these dormant treasures. He wondered whether he could compose anything as beautiful as the books themselves, and he thought of her lying on his lap.

"Writing stories in these books would be like giving birth," he thought, and had an image of her eyes opening on her ashen face.

"I want to buy these two," said Gentel.

"Yes, but the larger one is special," said Giorgio half aloud.

"I know. That's why I want it."

"Sorry," said Giorgio. "I cannot sell that one. The little one, sí."

Gentel was taken aback that Giorgio wouldn't sell one of the books in his store. "Really?" he said. "How strange, but if that's the way you feel…"

Gentel understood the difficulty of relinquishing a love of one's creation. These weren't just objects for sale, even if they were in a store; they were Giorgio's family, his loves. Gentel found another book to accompany the smaller one and bought the two.

Giorgio, also a bachelor, had a forlorn quality, a distant sadness that resonated with Gentel and gave an undercurrent of familiarity. Gentel came often to the bookstore over the next few months and they became friends. They spoke about soccer, politics and art. The two men bonded. Gentel, who was in need of a way to spend his time, became Giorgio's apprentice and learned to make books with empty pages.

When a customer wanted to buy one of Gentel's books many months later, Gentel hugged it against his chest, as

Giorgio had done. It was more than a book; it was a part of himself. The blank pages still needed to be filled.

"I'm sorry," said Gentel. "This one isn't for sale; it's special, and not quite finished yet. Can you find another?"

The customer looked annoyed, but Giorgio smiled at Gentel and nodded.

"How about *this* one?" the tourist asked. "How much is this one?"

Now it was Giorgio's turn. The book was one of his recent favorites on display. "This one, too, is not for sale," he said, joining his friend.

"Are you guys out of your mind? Isn't this a bookstore? How do you make any money?"

The customer stormed out and the two friends laughed.

Gentel had found a new home. He made large and small books with leather covers showing abstract designs, mostly curved lines of varying thickness in gold leaf, that glittered like Annie's hair in the sun when she was his little girl. Not having seen her for many, many years now, he didn't know whether her hair was still shiny blond. Probably it had lost its yellow luster, or perhaps she dyed it brown or ochre or…well…he didn't know. He'd lost touch after Rachel remarried and Annie had gone off to college. They faded into empty pages.

Some of Gentel's books had many pages, some few; some had pages of soft pink, like he remembered her toenails on the night of her murder; some had cream-colored pages, the color tone of her calf. Occasionally, he expressed his longings in his books. In one he fantasized that death extended a young, terminally ill woman's life by reincarnating her as a living spirit in a lonely man's heart. In another he wrote a poem in iambic pentameter about the freedom of shamans transforming from spirits to humans and back again, and in still another he wrote a short poem that didn't rhyme about the futility of sinister forces attempting to slay angels in heaven. He had no desire to publish his work or show it to anyone; they were as private as his imagination.

One day after many months Gentel told Giorgio about the murder. He confessed his guilt for not trying hard enough to save her, for being happy that the assailant ran away and left him alone with her, and how he gave his heart to the beautiful victim.

"She became an inseparable part of me, more than a wife," he said.

"I know it's strange, Giorgio. Rachel left, took Annie away, I was lonely…and you should have seen her. An angel. She'll live forever in my mind. How can one describe perfection? She was human art…she filled the void in me…the empty pages… and still does. I've lived with her…for twenty-five years…no, a few more than that."

"Why didn't you call the police or get an ambulance?"

"I yelled for help, looked around, but it was deserted. I didn't know where to go, didn't speak a word of Italian, and then I felt like an accomplice. I can't explain it. I wanted her for myself so badly. I thought she was dead…she must have been…I felt no pulse, no breath, no movement…well, after that final little flutter. Oh, God…I can't talk about it anymore."

Giorgio raised his eyebrows and shook his head in bewilderment.

The years flowed by without ripples. Gentel learned Italian, made books with empty pages and helped Giorgio restore ancient manuscripts. Although Gentel did not bring up the murder again, the leather covers of his books often revealed his memories and fantasies. In a few he drew the alley poorly lit by a single beam from an incandescent lamp, or misty with an angel floating under an arch. Once he showed a young man, himself, with her still alive. A brilliant yellow halo emanated from her short hair. On his favorite cover, she was lying on his lap asleep with a Mona Lisa smile. He kept these books on a shelf in his apartment. They were not for sale, and the collection grew as a shrine.

When the mused inspired him, he wrote short stories in the empty pages of his favorite books and moved them to another shelf.

He also made books for sale. These had abstract shapes on the covers, often appearing like cobblestones. They were displayed alongside Giorgio's books that were for sale. Occasionally, he would refuse to sell one of his books as a joke and the two comrades giggled when the customer left, perplexed and irritated.

One day Gentel made a book with a rose-colored cover, almost pink, embossed on the upper left corner with a knife with a wooden handle and curved blade. A silver plate etched faintly with the initials *A.P.* capped the handle. Dark red elongated drops dripped from the blade into a maroon pool on the pinkish background. The design had a grotesque quality that was painful for Gentel to look at and yet at the same time an abstract quality that was pleasing and similar to the designs covering the books he sold. He added the book to his private collection and each night when he came home he looked at the cover and ran his fingers along the handle of the knife, which was raised just enough from the background to give him a creepy, tactile sensation of déjà vu.

As the weeks passed, Gentel began obsessing about this book and rushed home early to feel the embossed knife. He dreamed about deep pools of blood that formed waves in the wind. His old dreams of handcuffs bearing his initials and a policeman interrogating him in a dark dungeon recurred. He thought of writing a murder story in the book, a whodunit mystery, but never found the energy. It didn't seem right. Fiction was not appropriate.

"I think I want to sell this," he told Giorgio one day as he placed the book on the counter. "Actually, I'm not sure. Can we keep it in the shop and see how I feel if someone wants to buy it? If I'm not here, let me know and I'll decide then. Okay?"

"What beautiful shades of red," said Giorgio. "Ah, the knife."

Gentel didn't respond and Giorgio looked at him knowingly.

"Could be," Gentel said. "It's whatever you want. Haven't you ever seen a figure emerge from shapes that stick in your mind, but you aren't sure if the artist meant it?"

"Of course. That even happens with my own designs! I like this book. Let's put it in the window for awhile."

The next day a short woman, mid-fiftyish, overweight, with a raspy voice and grey hair entered the shop. She had a sweet smile and a tiny dimple in her chin.

"Can I help you," asked Giorgio.

"Yes, please. These books are beautiful." She opened one in front of her and felt the soft texture of the hand-made, blank pages.

"You like?" asked Giorgio. "The empty pages are for you to make these books your own."

"Oh, they're precious. Did you make them?"

"Most, yes. Not all. An American colleague works with me now. He made some of these."

"An American?" she said and lowered her eyes.

"I love the abstract designs on the leather covers, like cobblestones on the old streets. I would like to write in these books. I write; stories, poems, thoughts."

"Really. These are made for you then," said Giorgio.

"The book in the window, with all the red, and the curved shape at the top, almost like a knife blade, did you make that one?"

"A very beautiful book. You have good taste. No, my American colleague made that one. He's not here now. He has a cold and is at home."

"How much is it?"

"He didn't say. He doesn't sell all the books he makes. He told me he wasn't sure about this one. I need to ask him. Would you be interested in any other book?"

"I like them all, but I really want that one. Would you call him and see if he'll agree to sell it?"

She went outside to look more closely at Gentel's book and when she returned Giorgio said, "I'm sorry to keep you waiting. My colleague had difficulty making up his mind. He says it's very personal and he won't sell it, at least not now. Please look around; you may find another that you like."

"I'm so sorry, so very sorry," she said. Her shoulders slumped. "I don't want any other right now. Do you think he might change his mind? Would you call me if he does?" She fidgeted. "Or you could give him my number and perhaps I can persuade him to sell it to me?"

"Of course. I'll talk to him. You say you are a writer?" asked Giorgio.

"Yes."

"I would like to read what you have published. Could you give me the titles?"

"Oh, no, no. I write, but never publish. That's why I like these books so much. They're so...personal and private. I always write with a pen, never a computer. I have never shown anyone what I write, not even my husband. Especially not my husband!"

"Why is that, may I ask?"

After an uncomfortable pause, she said, "I write to realize another person's dream...a man I never met. The books are not entirely mine. It's hard to explain. They're like a voice in the dark. Never mind."

She sighed. "Please don't forget to ask your American colleague about selling his book."

When she reached the doorway she added, "If he won't agree to sell it, please give him my phone number and ask him to call me. Maybe I will be able to persuade him."

Standing on the sidewalk, she looked at the book in the window for a long time. Giorgio watched as she rubbed her left side gently. She sighed again, saw Giorgio watching her, smiled sadly, and walked away.

"Tell him to call me," she muttered under her breath when she was out of range for him to hear.

Carved Stone

"One million three hundred thousand, do I hear one million four hundred thousand?"

"One four!" floated from the back of the room.

"Yes sir; one million four hundred thousand from the gentleman in the rear. Do I hear one million five hundred thousand for this powerful Tutuyea Ikkidluak carving? One million four hundred thousand going once… going twice…"

Except for special African pieces, ethnic art was relegated to the lower echelons of Sotheby's auctions. In the twentieth century, auctions of Arctic carvings were minor events attended by a handful of eccentric individuals who were not taken seriously in the art world. But that changed as the twenty-first century progressed, in large part due to Jane Simonton, the recluse who wrote scholarly treatises on her amazing collection of Inuit sculptures.

"One million five hundred thousand," came another bid.

"Thank you. We have one five. Do I hear one six? Going once at one million five hundred thousand…"

"ONE MILLION SIX HUNDRED THOUSAND!"

Mr. Lansing must have had the most extensive collection of impressionists, old master paintings and porcelains in the world. Inuit art was his new passion.

"One million six hundred thousand...going once... going twice," said the auctioneer, trying to retain his professional bearing.

"One million seven hundred thousand," came a quiet female voice from the sidelines.

"Did I hear one seven? Is that correct?" asked the auctioneer.

The thick air was silent.

"Yes."

"One million seven hundred thousand it is then," said the auctioneer. "Going once..."

"Two million," responded Mr. Lansing, making it clear he was going to buy this piece; price was not an issue.

The large, elderly bidder slumped her shoulders, her short iron-gray hair frizzing in the heat of the New York July afternoon.

The gavel came down as the auctioneer nodded to Mr. Lansing.

Unrecognized and unsuccessful in her bid, Jane Simonton turned and left the room, priced out of the market she had been instrumental in creating.

60 Years Earlier

Rain made Jane's thick, brown hair – so different from her mother's refined auburn silk hair – knot against her scalp. Jane took after her dark-haired father, a heavy set, bulky man who stood out among the fair-skinned Scandinavian types in St. Paul. Jane hated her curls, especially on wet days, when her mother tried to straighten them out with a stiff brush, making Jane feel ashamed of her looks. "Daddy likes my hair," she told her mother soon after he returned from Vietnam, when she was six years old.

Two years later, her father abandoned his family.

During recess on rainy days at school, the kids formed little cliques, the boys on one side of the room and the girls on the other. Jane felt like a stone pillar planted between them. She was at least half a head taller than the others, making it impossible to blend out of sight.

She often hung around Suzie, despite a clumsy feeling of not belonging. Jane wished she could be like Suzie, or Suzie Q as she was called, popular Suzie Q, sometimes just Q, and occasionally Quzie Sue by her best friends. Jane admired the way Suzie would wander over to the boys' side of the room and kick Jimmy in the shins and run back, looking like a comet with a brilliant yellow tail, taunting "got you Jimmy, in the shinny, Jimmy, got you good."

What Jane really wanted to do during recess was to play with Freddy, but he was always running around with his friends. He laughed a lot and used to dig his knuckles into his friends' heads, saying loud enough for everyone around to hear, "take that, gutter rat!" Then he would dash away as fast as he could and do a funny little dance at a safe distance, challenging his victim to catch him.

Jane didn't have Suzie's courage to run over and kick Freddy's shins. But Jane didn't want to anyway. She wanted to run over and kiss him on the cheek. She never did, of course, but she thought about it a lot. Her love was safer from a distance.

When adolescence came she watched Freddy flirt with Suzie Q, now just Sue, who was elected class president. When Sue winked at Freddy as she displayed her nubile body as a cheerleader, Jane looked the other way. There was no way Jane could be a cheerleader. She was too tall, her hair too frizzy, her love of ice cream too great; it showed. She immersed herself in her studies.

After high school, Jane went to the state college in out-of-the-way Lake Point, Minnesota to study art. She loved paintings, particularly portraits of beautiful people, and envisioned being a museum curator. As in high school, she felt self-conscious among her peers. They were thin and attracted boys, who pretended to do homework at the art library in order to meet them. Jane went there too, but never met anyone. She watched the others flirt and blended into the background as a blur of bland gray.

Jane changed her major to math. It came easily to her and made her feel safe. The boys ignored math majors, eliminating competition in a battle-free zone. From math she drifted to computers, which boded well for employment after graduation. As the daughter of a divorced, single mother, she wanted to prepare for the eventuality of a lonely life after school.

In computer class she met the only boy she dated in college. She was drawn to how different Ferdinand – an inch shorter than her 5 foot ten inches – looked from the other boys. He was socially clumsy, like her, and had one brown eye and one light blue, and had asymmetrically placed ears: the right was higher than the left and protruded, as if collected at random from a pile of discards and pinned on as an afterthought. He was frail and as unsuited to be an athlete as she was to be a cheerleader. An albino with white hair and eyebrows, he hid from the sun as much as she hid in dim corners.

Jane felt pretty in Ferdinand's company.

One evening, after a stroll around the lake, they stood outside her dormitory when Ferdinand said, "I like you," leaned towards her and clumsily put his lips on hers. She recoiled, unaccustomed to being touched and never having been kissed by a boy before.

"Are you all right?" he asked. "Did I do something wrong? I'm sorry. I thought..."

"No. I mean, nothing's wrong. I don't know. I don't want to talk about it. I'm sorry too. I need to go home. Please. I'll see you tomorrow in class."

"Are you sure?" he said, his face flushed, and walked her back to her dormitory.

"Oh, god," she muttered, back in her room. She lay face down on her unmade bed, felt the chill of ice crystallizing around her heart, and pulled the sheet over her head.

Ferdinand did not come to class the following week. Illness, he said. They remained friends for the rest of the year; that was the best either of them could accomplish. Contact with flesh was not her forte.

After graduation Jane became a computer programmer in a small company in Lake Point, rose quickly and made a substantial salary, which she judiciously saved. She had become part of the dark matter of society.

She moved into a relatively large apartment in the edge of town. She loved the expanse of the living room, which she kept unfurnished. The space was liberating, almost like being in the wilderness.

On Sundays she often went to the college museum, which occasionally had interesting exhibits. There was a small portrait by a local artist that she never failed to visit. She usually sat on the bench directly facing it, and squinted to focus on the mask-like face, pale, like Ferdinand's. She had lost touch with him after graduation, and his absence nourished her sadness.

Her favorite painting in the museum was a complex battle scene that evoked a sexual response. The painting showed victorious soldiers wielding swords, injured and dying warriors, rapes and rearing horses, and a floating castle in the background. She liked its outrageousness – a visual collection of moods that didn't fit together – and that no one knew the name of the painter. Without the crutch of a reputable artist, the scene had to stand on its own merits, like she felt she had to do. Also, the various characters in the picture gave her a vicarious thrill of danger – excitement without threat – and the floating castle, well, that was a dream.

An exhibit on Inuit sculptures was slated to open on her twenty-fourth birthday. She went to the library to familiarize herself with these works of art from Northern Canada. At first, she was not impressed. She found the many bears and seals and walruses repetitious and ordinary, and the shamans – part human, part animal – nonsensical mixtures. The names of the artists were impossible to pronounce so they might as well have been unknown or fictional. But, she thought, wasn't that what she liked about the battle scene painting she loved, it's independence?

Jane bought a book on Inuit carvings, and then another. There was something lonely and stark about the Arctic, a foreignness that appealed to her. Also, despite the similar subjects, the voice of the artists transcended the subject matter; some were meticulously realistic and detailed, others abstract and expressive. She was drawn to a photograph of a whalebone sculpture of a shaman with wild hair, impaled by a spear, a gaping mouth and bird-like feet. She had mingled repulsion and fascination of these shaman and their powers over life and death. Her mind flipped back and forth between the speared shaman and the battle scene, both worlds of fantasy and lust and violence, emotions her life lacked. Sometimes she imagined Ferdinand, white as snow, as an Inuit wandering across desolate fields of pristine white snow reflecting brilliant sunshine.

Jane also loved the myths behind the Inuit sculptures. One of her favorites was that of the Sedna, or mermaid, about a young girl transformed into a goddess after being rescued from an island by her father from her cruel, mythical husband. When her husband discovered his wife had been kidnapped, he changed into a bird and flew over the water to find her in her father's boat. He flapped his wings violently, creating turbulence on the sea threatening to overturn the small craft. Her father threw her overboard to save himself and the boat from capsizing. When she clung to the side of the boat, he cut off her fingers bit by bit until she sank to the bottom of the sea. Horrible, yes, but the story continues: the pieces of her fingers gave birth to all the marine mammals, and she transformed into the Sedna, the goddess who ruled the creatures of the seas.

The myth of becoming a goddess despite a cruel husband and father's rejection had a personal quality for Jane.

The exhibition opened on a Wednesday morning. Few people were expected until the evening reception. Jane wanted to be the first to see the exhibit.

"I won't be in today," she told her boss, calling in sick. She felt guilty about lying, but gave herself the present of a day off. It was her birthday, after all. Her only other gift was a card sent by her mother that had arrived two days earlier.

No card or present from her father. She wondered whether he even remembered it was her birthday. She certainly couldn't count on him to be rescued.

Jane entered the exhibit with her eyes closed. She wanted the full impact of the art in one blow, like having her knuckles chopped off.

"Oh!" she exclaimed when she opened her eyes. Many pieces were larger than she expected, and more powerful. Also, the books had failed in showing the multiple shades of color and veins of the stones. The dark green serpentine rocks showed browns and whites and yellows. Many pieces appeared rough and unfinished; others shiny and polished. Some were gray, a few white marble, and one, a muskox, very pale green.

She was most impressed with the sense of movement. What a paradox – mobility emanating from anchored stones. A large shaman bird with extended wings and a human face appeared to be swooping down as if to deliver a message. The teeth on a swimming bear were so menacing that Jane retreated a few steps.

She walked through the three rooms of the exhibit many times, stopping in front of a goose with an extended neck and gaping mouth. She stopped breathing for an instant to achieve absolute quiet, as she imagined it might be on a windless day in the Arctic tundra, and was angry at her heart for interrupting the serenity with its incessant beating, reminding her of the uncontrolled thumping of her heart when Ferdinand placed his lips on hers.

Jane went to work the next day glowing like an expectant mother.

"I recuperate quickly," she told her boss. He said nothing, but his secretary, Barbara, one of Jane's few if distant friends, shot Jane a hint of a smile.

Jane studied the carvings for the next two weekends and they became so alive in her mind, so transformed into friends, that she wondered whether they were as excited to see her, as she was to see them.

A shaman muskox head with huge, carved horns on his human-like face projected uncanny power. He was like a humorous king who reigned over the other pieces, with his distorted mouth, crooked nose, short fang-like teeth and oddly shaped, expressive eyes. This aristocratic piece also gave her a sense of security, as if he was there to make sure everything was safe and in order. His strong presence made her feel like part of his harem, and inspired complex feelings she found difficult to put in words.

In short, the carvings achieved life in her presence.

When the exhibit ended, Jane could not free her mind of the Inuit carvings. She kept the book containing the picture of the impaled shaman on the living room floor, where it remained open. It initiated her collection: one picture of one carving, a vey small collection, indeed. The open space of the unfurnished room was its territory, its Arctic grandeur, and when Jane realized the meaning of this, she knew what to do.

"I would like to take a few days for vacation," she told her boss the next day. "I need a break. Is okay?"

Two days later, she was standing in front of *The Warm Igloo* in Montreal, when a middle-aged man smiled at her through the display window and waved her in. Bells jangled when she walked across the threshold.

This was no exhibit; these pieces could become hers. She could assemble a following of her own, like a goddess. Although she had never actually bought a carving, she considered herself a collector. Ownership was but a step in the process. She lifted a kneeling yellow-green serpentine caribou with gently sloping antlers off the shelf, placing her left hand under the animal's belly.

"It could be *mine*," she said without words, and immediately the sculpture no longer looked the same. It became hers, because she willed it so.

"You have a good eye," said the gallery owner. "It's one of my favorite carvings. I am going to miss it."

Jane walked back to her hotel, cradling the sculpture in her hands, and set it on the chest of drawers in the room. She turned it to the right, then the left, dropping her head in the opposite direction each time as if she were dancing with it, her sculpture: her's.

"I love it," she thought, and wished she had someone to tell, like Ferdinand.

Artic Images was crowded and more commercial than *The Warm Igloo*. A young salesman pounced upon her.

"Can I help you?" he asked.

"I'm just looking," she said in a muffled voice, avoiding eye contact.

"Please, go ahead. What type of carvings are you interested in? Large ones? Small ones?"

"Any kind. I'm just looking around, if you don't mind," she answered, visibly annoyed. She was a collector and was hunting, like the Inuit, and didn't need help. She headed toward an inviting Sedna with long braided hair covering her back and tail. When a Sedna had well-coiffed hair, all was well with the world: the fishing was good, the sea mammals abundant. The Sedna was a provider that would deliver. Messy hair symbolized bad times – poor fishing.

This was a good time for Jane.

She bought several small sculptures: a drum dancer whose tongue was sticking out, a sign of trance-like involvement; a spirit figure with bulging eyes; and a standing caribou straining its neck upward to sniff the environment. She was sniffing the environment, in her own way.

She also purchased a large polar bear sculpture, upright on two bowed legs, with its feet turned inwards, looking awkward like the bashful grade-school girl she had been. One arm was limp against its body, seemingly injured, while the other was raised to its face with the paw scratching the chin, as if the bear was thinking.

Jane thought the bear was planning the future, pondering its next home, her home.

On her last shopping day, Jane purchased a black stone carving of an alert mother owl with a chick clutching on her back. The carving had entered her mind and latched on the minute she saw it. The piece had chosen her, not the other way around.

On the drive home, Jane placed the sculptures on the back seat, except for the big polar bear, which she protected by the seat belt on the seat next to her.

"Polo," she said – she called him that – "I can't wait to show you my living room. You'll love it. There's so much space for you there."

She bounced up the stairs and into her apartment holding the spirit figure in one hand and the kneeling caribou in the other and placed them on the floor in the bare living room. Before fetching the other carvings, she moved the two pieces to no less than six different spots in the empty living room and, finally, left them side-by-side by the bay window. Excited, she brought up the others, one by one, and placed them all in a circle in the middle of the room. She struggled with Polo because he was he was so heavy. She brought the two by the window into the fold and sat cross-legged in the center of the circle with all the pieces facing her.

It was like a scene from camp, with the counselor in the center of the circle caring for the campers. She walked around the inside of the circle of sculptures, then circled the outside, went through the center, and moved to the edge of the room, sat down and faced her new family from a distance. Every position gave her a different perspective.

"Now you're home; I'm your mother and am here for you. Our family will grow," she told them, feeling happier than she had ever been in her life.

The next day Jane broke up the circle of sculptures and placed pieces in different parts of the room, and in different combinations. She treated them as equals, but in truth she loved Polo most of all, and her heart melted for the baby owl embracing its mother. She spent hours arranging and rearranging the carvings. Sometimes just changing the direction that they faced brought out a different character trait and distinct personality.

Six months later Jane went to Vancouver on another buying spree. She bought four sensational carvings in *The Mystic Explorer*, including a violent scene of a falcon sinking its sharpened claws into a weasel. She could almost hear the screams of desperation from the hunted prey.

"Life," she sighed, as she scooped it up and made it hers. "And death."

In another gallery she bought a sitting wolf looking up at the sky, as if searching for stars.

Jane continued to rearrange the carvings, experimenting with various groupings, cliques she called them, but her living room was turning into a crowd and she feared their individuality would be lost. She decided to have a carpenter add shelves. What was she to do as her family continued to grow, which she knew it would? I must sell some, she thought; there must be turnover. However, she scanned the collection, each piece a part of her soul, a member of her family.

"I can't," she concluded. She lacked the strength to chop off their fingers, which were the same as her fingers. She could never be a Sedna.

The shelves were added in the living room and then in the adjacent room, extending her collection. Three years went by and she became a matriarch over a family of stone, an extraordinary collection comprising over a hundred carvings. This was her love and her life, her private empire. She was a Sedna after all, a different kind of Sedna, one that provided for herself rather than the community.

No one had yet seen Jane's reclusive collection, so one day she invited Barbara to her apartment.

Barbara came on Friday night, bringing her brother. Richard was thirty-five and unmarried. Jane was irritated by the imposition, but flattered and excited at the same time, since it seemed obvious this was an introduction and the closest thing to a date since Ferdinand.

"Wow!" exclaimed Richard, when they walked into Jane's apartment. Neither he nor Barbara knew where to look first. They went from bears to whales to spirit figures. Richard glided through the collection, caressing the pieces with the tips of his fingers. Jane thought his hand was like a soft pillow against the hard stone.

"Do you mind if I touch them?" he asked after the fact.

"Oh, no! They must be felt. They want to be touched. "

Jane stood aside as her guests became acquainted with her family. Her knees shook and her stomach churned, conflicted between ecstasy and trepidation. As much as she relished center stage, she also felt invaded. The collection was inseparable from her, and she felt assaulted, as if her guests were trespassing into her private life, and she wanted them out. Yet, at the same time, the collected stone glowed in their presence, and she basked in that glow. The scene turned an empty theater into a vibrant production, complete with actors and captivated audience.

"This running bear by Pauta Saila is a gem," she said, very much the expert docent. "Look at the four teeth, a powerful innovation by this artist. "Yes, that's a wonderful peaceful caribou. You have good taste. Osuitok Ipeelie carved it. He's one of the original masters. Look here! It's a tiny drum dancer by Silas Kayakjuak. So expressive!! Touch it! You'll *feel* the movement. Over here the falcon is killing the weasel. Powerful, no?

It's by Tutuyea Ikkidluak. His is a tragic story – killed himself at twenty-eight. He got very depressed after being sent off to school in southern Canada by the missionaries. When he returned to the Arctic he didn't fit anymore. Such a gift he had! The stone projects his intensity. The little ivory muskox? Mannasie Akpaliapik made it. What a treasure! There's so much movement expressed. Oh, yes, that one. Judas Ullulag was the artist. What a humorous, original sculpture, don't you think? Crazy eyes, wouldn't you say? I'm in love with that head. The whole village in that little boat, which is called a umiak, is by Joanassie Faber. The people are spearfishing. It's more than a good carving. It's a metaphor for cooperation to survive in the harsh Arctic. Latholassie Akesuk, David Ruben Piquoken. These are all great and important Inuit carvers, although essentially no one in the conventional world of art has ever heard of them."

Then she paused a moment. "I'll change that, maybe," she continued, with a lower voice, as much to herself as to Barbara and Richard.

"Sorry, I'm talking too much," Jane muttered, but she couldn't stop. She explained every carving. "A few of these carvings have been damaged," she said, "but look how they have been restored and remain alive and well. The repairs are badges of honor and signs of love."

"No one knows who made this little bird looking so sad," she said, and she picked it up tenderly. "I love anonymity. It's a trace of human expression that transcends the person who made it. It floats in its own universe."

As soon as these words escaped Jane's lips she felt she had just described herself, and she paused momentarily in embarrassment. But then she stroked the long hair of the thin stone Sedna next to her and felt comforted.

"I like your collection," said Richard. "Impressive."

"Thanks."

"Do you like wild blackberries?" Richard asked.

"I love them."

"They're my favorite fruit," he said, "especially when they're warm from the sun. I know a place not far from here where you can pick them. Would you like to come with me tomorrow and get some?"

Barbara moved to leave, but Richard lagged behind.

"Ten o'clock?" he said.

Richard arrived at precisely ten the next morning.

During the drive Jane asked Richard about himself.

"I'm a veterinarian," he said.

They hiked up a mountainside until they found patches of blackberry bushes. They filled three baskets, eating two for each one they collected. The backs of their hands made contact from time to time as they walked.

"Are you ever curious to see polar bears or caribou or any of the magnificent wildlife in the Arctic, especially since you're a vet?" she asked.

"It's too barren up there. I'm happy here," he said.

Lucky guy, she thought, and was overcome by a passing moment of sadness.

"Are you okay? You got quiet suddenly."

She nodded, but remained silent. Ferdinand's image flashed in her mind.

He took her hand in his.

"I'm so tired," she said, not knowing what broke the spell.

She racked her mind for topics to talk about on the drive home. Whatever made it so easy and natural to be with Richard a few hours ago had slipped away.

When they reached her apartment he touched her cheek. "I hope you feel better," he said.

"Thanks. I'll be all right. I...I better go in now."

Would she? She felt heavy, like stone.

He said they could spend time together another day, and she agreed, but she knew better. She watched him from the window head back to his car and drive away. The street was empty and covered with the evening dusk.

It was deathly quiet in the apartment by herself. She placed her hand upon her cheek where Richard had touched her and held it there. She walked into the living room to be among her carvings, stroked Polo on his back, and headed for the caribou. "You would have loved the little stream," she told him.

Her voice broke the solitude and comforted her. She looked out the bay window and saw the stars twinkling in the cold galaxy.

"They're so far away," she thought.

She turned and walked from sculpture to sculpture, circling each piece.

"I love you all," she said.

The room was filled with her stone family, perched on stands and the floor and shelves. She found a spot beside the wolf with a Sedna on one side of her and a bear on the other. She sat and leaned her head against the owl with its chick behind her, being careful not to push too hard. A mist of tears brought fog and made the falcon's wings a few carvings away from her quiver. The brave hunter in the back of the room launched his spear with a steady movement of his arm. The white stands mocking ice floes drifted as if on water, moving first apart and then back together, squeezing space, carrying their load without concern.

"Carved stone," she thought. "That's all they are, and yet, my life, my loves."

She sat among the carvings, as one of them. Who's alive? she wondered, and who is not?

"Time for bed," she said quietly, but when she looked ahead and right and left, all passages seemed blocked by sheets of ice and dangerous animals. There was no mercy in the air and no way out.

When she glanced out the window, gathering clouds hid the stars.

She closed her eyes and surrendered to sleep. She dreamed of birds flying in the sky and of caribou with snouts up high, their antlers glistening in the sun. There were seals and fish and whales as well, and shaman transforming from man to beast and back again. She wrapped her arm around the solid owl, now her pillow and bedfellow, and squeezed it just a little. She brushed her lips against its wings and snuggled up as best she could. She sensed the morning on its way, but now was night, the world was hers, and so she slept and slept and dreamed some more.

Less Is Not Enough

We all have our inner voice – private, teasing, often cruel – that taunts with tunes so personal we dare not sing the words aloud. Poor Sylvia Slender, even trimmer than her name, was often bruised in battle with her inner voice – until she won the war.

"Paint! Paint! And more paint! It's so busy, so many colors, swirls everywhere, looks like a mess up close. The only thing he got rid of was his ear. Ha, ironic," Sylvia whispered to her classmate as Van Gogh's 'The Starry Night' flashed on the screen. This was the last lecture of her art major before graduation. It couldn't happen too soon for her.

"Note the movement of the sky generated by the brush strokes and interplay of blues and yellows, and how the dominant green tree in the foreground towers over the sleeping town and joins the stars, Godlike, and in harmony with the shorter, central, slim steeple among the little houses. All nature seems alive as the people hide until morning in their homes, whose windows glow with a yellow light. Where is this town? Maybe only in Van Gogh's mind, a secret forever, and…" Dr. Warlock lectured on and on and on.

"Yakkity yak, blah blah blah blah. His words are making me nauseous. There isn't a tiny piece of white canvas showing. Such a waste of paint. So inefficient! Look, even that big green tree Dr. Warlock loves so much is weighted down with heavy rust-colored lines," Sylvia hissed. "Old Vincent was good, I admit it, but don't you just want to strip some of those parallel lines away? They're like bars. Just looking at it makes me feel imprisoned. Everything seems so heavy, Joanie, know what I mean?"

"Shhh!!! Jesus, Sylvia, look who's yaking."

"Sylvia, do you want to share your opinion with us on this masterpiece?" Dr. Warlock looked annoyed.

Sylvia blushed. "I was saying…that is…I think…well, it's a great painting, of course…but I…think it's just too…"

"Too what, Sylvia?"

"Too BUSY!"

A murmur rippled through the classroom, followed by a few giggles from the back.

"Too BUSY, Sylvia?"

"Sorry, but I think so. Makes me dizzy. I'm just being honest."

One month later, Sylvia's mother watched proudly as her daughter was called forth to receive her college diploma, and magna cum laude at that. Sylvia's college years hadn't been easy. Twice she left school, once for a year and a half when she was treated for anorexia. She dropped out again for three months to spend time with her mother after the divorce. Sylvia missed her father a lot. He never called her and had sent only one postcard from somewhere in the Caribbean:

"Sorry Syl, life is short you know, had to cut the fluff. Love you. Dad."

She used to talk to him about many things, about poetry and crime, and the line between art and science. She loved when he read his stories to her, the ones he hoped to publish, but was hurt when she found them crumpled in the trash if she had made a critical comment.

Sylvia was a star on the track team in high school. "Thin people can fly," she told her teammates. She was incredibly fast, propelled her tiny feet moving back and forth like a mechanical toy. "I hate the clutter of people in front of me," she said. "I just love open space in front of me."

One day in the heat of competition, she was so far in front that she looked behind and saw space there too. No clutter front or back! She kept her eye on the other girls struggling to catch up, and the next thing she knew she was in the hospital.

"Where am I?" she asked when she opened her eyes and saw the fuzzy outline of the nurse changing an intravenous bag of nourishment.

"You ran into a pole, sweetheart, and whamo," the nurse said. You got a dozen stitches above your right eye."

Sylvia touched her forehead gently. "Ouch!"

"See what I mean? Just relax. You're going to be all right."

You idiot, said her inner voice, meaning herself.

Sylvia suffered no lasting damage and, a few years later at her college graduation, the scar was almost invisible on her pretty face.

Sylvia was breathtaking. The purity of her skin made fresh white snow look dusty. When she smiled, her blue-green eyes glowed. The three tiny dimples on her cheeks, one on the right and two on the left, were balanced by a slight rightward tilt of her head. She bore a small notch at the edge of her right nostril like a subtle badge of honor, implying she had paid her genetic dues.

Her father had loved best her long, soft, wavy, red hair.

"Red velvet," he called it. "Never let scissors near these red hot flames. It's a fire for all the world to see, my little girl, my spark."

Sylvia was barely five feet tall.

But it was not her beauty or her running speed that ruled her life. And it was not her father who obsessed her: it was her relentless inner voice. When her father admired her hair, her inner voice would say, *What's with this hair thing? Fire is just overheated air that singes and destroys. It's nothing more than decoration in a fireplace that gives off heat and disappears when the logs are gone.*

After a discouraging hunt for employment, Sylvia was ecstatic when she finally heard, "Well, Ms. Slender, we're pleased to make you an offer."

"Thank you, Mr. Goldschmidt!" she beamed. "When should I start?"

Come on, dummy. How much moolah?

"What will my salary be?" she asked timidly.

"Let's start at $30 an hour, and 5 percent of the price for each sale."

Better sell a lot, baby doll.

Goldschmidt's Gallery was well known in Chicago. Sylvia had never sold art and didn't realize selling art was about selling, not art.

"It's a fine painting, exactly the kind you are looking for: a landscape by an up and coming young artist. Doesn't the red sunset look real?" she said to Mr. Chalmer's on his third visit to the gallery. She hoped he would be her first paying customer.

Looks like shit, railed her voice in an unrelenting battle with clutter. *Shit, shit, shit. That's why there's so much brown in it.*

"I don't know. It's not quite right. The colors are dull. Got anything else by this painter? I do like his style."

Got part of that right, buster, it's not quite right. Brighter colors? You must be kidding.

Her inner voice was on a rampage. *Quiet, quiet, quiet,* she begged, and then she smiled.

"Just a moment. I think I have just what you want."

Sylvia disappeared. Five minutes later she brought out a landscape of tree-covered hills with flowers and squirrels in the foreground. The thick, brilliantly colored paint made her nauseous.

Horrible, horrible, h-o-r-r-i-b-l-e! shouted that all-pervasive monster inside her gorgeous head.

"Mr. Chalmer, what do you think of this? It's called "Wondrous Nature." Sylvia made up the title.

Don't push it, baby doll. My god, what a M-O-N-S-T-R-O-S-I-T-Y!

"The artist, Albert Switzer, is about 40 years old, lives in Portland, Maine, very... nouveau. Look for him in the art magazines," Sylvia said softly.

Nouveau? Get real.

"I love it. You have wonderful taste. It has such strong colors. Force and harmony. Movement and balance. Yes, everything I was looking for. 'Wondrous Nature', what a perfect name. The man's an artist, no question."

"The price is very attractive too since he's relatively undiscovered; $4,500," she said. "I understand some of his paintings went for over $8,000 last year in his one-man show. She made that up too. This is a bargain since it's an early work. Don't you love the little squirrels?"

"Squirrels? I thought they were rabbits. Yes, you're right, squirrels. I'll take it. It's perfect for the den next to the bird cage."

"Good choice, Mr. Chalmer."

Her inner voice did a little jig, singing, *Yes, Yes, Y-E-S! $225 in the bank! Good work Sylvia, baby doll. Hooked your first big fish with that pile of paint as bait.*

And then the voice changed its tune.

God, what an ugly picture. It's so busy, busy.

Suddenly she imagined her father's face, smiling at her. *Good job, Syl! Nice work*, he said, kidnapping her inner voice as his own.

Sylvia hated when he did that, but at least that was some contact with him.

"Do you want to take the painting now, Mr. Chalmer, or should I have it delivered to your home?"

"I'll take it now. Want to surprise the little woman, know what I mean?"

"She'll be so excited."

Bet his 'little woman' is big as a tank, huge, gigantic, a steam-roller. Little, little, little. I could tell him a thing or two about little. Bet she eats like a horse!

"Thanks a lot, Mr. Chalmer. Come again soon," said Sylvia.

Yeah, soon, soon, soon.

Sylvia decided to buy a print for her new apartment to celebrate her first sale. As she considered what she might purchase, her inner voice weighed in again.

Don't tell me you're going to spoil these clean white walls with pictures.

She looked at the bare wall in front of her and saw endless possibilities. She imagined pictures of sexy men with hairy chests heaving hay with pitchforks; she saw hummingbirds flitting between branches so quickly it made her dizzy; she saw layers of white on white, making the wall as deep and mysterious as the ocean; she saw waves, which made her seasick. What to do? Leave the bare walls alone, or clutter them with pictures. In the morning she decided to shop for a print.

"How about this one?" asked the salesman as he showed her a monotype print of flowers with a bright blue background.

"No, I don't like it. Do you have one that's less busy, perhaps with more to think about and less to see?"

She went from gallery to gallery. Nothing satisfied her, and the more she saw the more impatient she became. She looked at impressionists, German expressionists and finally abstractionists. Jackson Pollock disgusted her.

She bought nothing. When she came home she thought the clean white walls looked beautiful and restful. She watched a gorgeous sunset in her mind against an imaginary horizon on the left side of the blank wall. On the right side, whales were spouting mists of seawater that formed a rainbow in the sunshine. She never found her cluttered mind too busy.

She drifted off to a dreamless state surrounded by four bare white walls filled with exciting adventures and poetic thoughts buried within her.

Weeks went by and the walls continued to serve as screens for her fantastic imaginings.

Then one day a handsome young customer with a ponytail pinched at the base with a rubber band walked in the gallery. His brown eyes scanned the pictures as he spoke to her.

Hang on, baby doll, he may be cute and all that, but...he's a customer, probably married or living with someone.

"I'm trying to cheer up my apartment," said Mr. Ponytail. "I'm in med school and need some art to brighten my life. What do you have that's inspiring and cheap?"

Damn. Cheap.

"Cheap, eh?" she responded. "I know what you mean. I've been trying to fix up my place for months and am not getting anywhere. Maybe I'll have better luck with yours! How about a blank canvas with the word 'cheap' written in small letters in one corner?"

He smiled.

She blanched. Even her inner voice was speechless for a few seconds.

Blank canvas. That's authentic art.

"Are you okay? Why don't you sit down? You look pale."

"Thanks. I'll just sit here for a second. Sorry, I don't know what came over me," she lied.

Color came back to her face. "I'm feeling better now. I'll go get a few prints for us to start finding something you might like. Be right back."

She found a variety of etchings, woodprints, and drawings stashed behind a big box in a corner of the storeroom. Apparently these didn't have much of a market. They were from the gallery's collection of minimalists and had, at most, a few lines of different shapes. The most extensive was an empty circle with squiggles outside the perimeter.

Wow. Less is more, hey baby doll. You can't complain that these are too busy.

"These don't make much sense to me, but I like them," said the young man.

Sylvia nodded in agreement with him and her inner voice.

They examined the small collection, he rubbing his chin in thought, she absorbing their simplicity. There was just enough on the plain sheets to remind her that someone else made these pieces of art, but not so much that she couldn't become part of it herself.

"I'd like this one, with the two red lines across the upper left corner and the blue dot in the lower right," the customer said.

Sylvia wrapped the print and thanked him as he gestured thumbs up going out the door.

I told you so. Lesser is better. Let the viewer be the artist.

Sylvia bought four minimalist prints from the gallery's collection, with her inner voice's consent. One had faint colors;

the others were in shades of gray. She gave free reign to her imagination to interpret their meaning.

Of course, baby doll. What do you expect? The artists are lazy. They want you to decide what they mean.

She was angry at her obtrusive inner voice for suggesting that she didn't know that. She knew that the white walls in her apartment were minimalist art, depending on her imagination and what *she* saw when she looked at them. No artist – no one – was telling her what to think or feel. She was the artist.

She experimented with the prints by placing them in different contexts: one per corner, or all lined up next to one another, or placed as a small square in the center of the wall, or off to one side. Each arrangement brought out different qualities of the prints and each arrangement made the room *feel* different. The square in the center made the room formal, each in a corner gave symmetry without formality, and the straight line of prints in the lower left corner along the floor was just plain funky and made her laugh at its absurdity.

Absurd as your empty life, absurd, absurd, absurd, screamed her inner voice.

Sylvia started to modify in her mind each painting and print she saw in the gallery; stripping color, erasing parts of figures, such as a lady's hat or a gentleman's necktie, and sometimes creating a grotesque figure that fascinated her. Occasionally she added something – a pair of glasses on an elderly gentleman reading a newspaper, or a dog at his side – but generally she deleted. She loved to delete, to take away the unnecessary clutter. She felt a new sense of power and pleasure. She wasn't selling art anymore; she was creating it in her mind.

Sylvia blossomed. She started dating and making friends. She looked prettier than ever as she wore less jewelry and makeup, allowing the natural beauty of her face and tiny body to shine.

One evening after a few glasses of wine at a dinner with a handsome date, Sylvia started explaining her attraction to less and to re-arrangement, stressing how the best art is in the mind of the beholder, and how she resented artists who imposed their feelings on others.

"But isn't self-expression what it's all about? How can you call a blank canvas art?" asked her date.

"No, no, you don't understand! The blank canvas is nothing. It's what I see in it."

"Oh, I get it," Mr. Charming said.

Bullshit. He doesn't get squat. Nice lips, chiseled chin, but inside, blank, B-L-A-N-K. Rearrange his symmetrical face, baby doll. Ha!!

Sylvia started to laugh.

"What's so funny?'

"Nothing," she said.

Her inner voice wouldn't let her sleep that night. At three in the morning it was still going strong.

You can't just bury all your thoughts, baby doll. You gotta have someone understand you. Your brain's connected to the world you know. Your body is too. You're not floating alone in space. Give it a rest. Quit fighting.

And then her inner voice transformed into a pencil undulating to jazzy, sexy music, a strip dance where it peeled away layers of wood and got thinner and thinner, and then began to write on a blank sheet of paper.

Sylvia squinted to read what it was writing: *fight, bite, CUT!* The pencil flipped expertly and now a big eraser was visible against the paper and swept across the written words. Blank paper re-emerged and sparkled white, so bright that she opened her eyes and saw the rising sun beaming light through the window onto her face.

It was time to get up and go to the gallery. She started to think about writing for the first time.

Sylvia started to write with a pencil, as in her dream. She loved the tactile nature of a pencil, even more than a pen. Writing with a computer was too mechanical for her taste. She wrote imaginative, surrealistic stories, mostly about loss. One was about a dandelion whose stem dissolved in tears when its seeds blew away. In another, the hopes of a little girl, who had dreamed of becoming a great runner, were dashed when a car crushed her foot. The driver was an Olympic track star. Still another was about twin girls, one an extrovert with irresistible charm, naïve and lovable, the other malicious and dominant with a soft voice that eroded her twin sister like a relentless eraser. Their father, who had deserted them, wrote long soulful letters to his mean daughter, and short jokes on postcards to the other.

Sylvia's inner voice remained relatively quiet during this new experimental transition. But she felt it lurking on the sidelines, waiting. And then one day, it broke the silence.

You don't care about writing, baby doll. Come on, be honest! All those words cluttering a clean white page? Horrible.

That pesky inner voice impressed her. Her enthusiasm dampened with each additional line she wrote, and when there was more dark than light on the page, she became irritable and started erasing. Each line that crumbled away with tiny bits of rubber satisfied her. Also, when the story unfolded on paper it felt too... *busy*...too explicit. She experimented with writing single phrases, and then single words in place of whole sentences, but nothing gave her the same satisfaction as seeing the words erased, with nothingness reappearing, and having the story remain in her lovely head.

You're a serious case, baby doll, said her inner voice one day as she erased three complete pages at the expense of seven pencil top erasers. As an author, she wasn't a minimalist; she was an executioner, a surgeon, a gravedigger. Sylvia closed her eyes and saw her inner voice once more as an undulating pencil, writing with red letters: *do/undo; build/smash; kiss/bite; write/erase; author/editor.*

EDITOR!

Editors revise, re-arrange, add, subtract, delete.

As an editor, baby doll, you can do to others as you do to yourself, as your father did to you: CUT!

Mr. Goldschmidt, she told him, I'm quitting. Sorry to be so abrupt. No, it's nothing you did. You have been very fair. Thanks so much. I'm…I'm going to be… an *editor.*

"An editor! How did you decide that?"

"I don't have a job yet. I don't know. I just love to re-arrange, to eliminate stuff. I like less, to trim…*slender…*"

Don't get cute, now, baby doll. Time to shut up.

"I tried writing, but…it didn't work. The more I wrote, the less I wanted to write. But…well, this sounds silly…I love to erase."

"What do you mean?"

"I like skeletons and space. I feel bombarded with any type of clutter, even in many of the paintings I'm selling. I'm sorry, but it's true."

Feels good to be honest, doesn't it, baby doll?

"If you could stay one more week it would be helpful," said Mr. Goldschmidt. "I can manage after that. Good luck, Sylvia. I hope you find what you're looking for."

"Ms. Slender…"

"Sylvia, please," she said to the tough looking woman interviewing her.

"Sylvia, you're inexperienced and have a lot to learn, but I have a good feeling about you. Are you willing to work hard?" asked Ms. Chiller.

Don't blow it, baby doll. Be cool. Answer the stupid question nicely.

"Oh, yes! I'll work very hard. You can count on me."

"Sally. All my employees call me Sally. We're a family. Welcome to *WriteStuff.*"

Sylvia thrived as an editor as she trimmed, cut, slashed. In one issue of the literary magazine she persuaded Sally to publish an anonymous piece (by herself of course) called "The Sadness of It All." It consisted of the title followed by two blank pages. At the bottom right of the second page was a period signifying the end of the story. The following issue contained a series of letters saying in various ways it was the greatest article the magazine had ever published. One claimed it had changed his life, giving him the courage to fill in the space with his own dreams. However, another wrote to say they were all morons and she was going to cancel her subscription.

Good going, baby doll, said her inner voice, as she read the letters. *But you're a total fake. Open your closet and take a look-see. Go live in a nudist colony if you don't need clothes. Yeah, yeah, yeah, tough bitch. Why do you need all that flaming fire on your head, combing it all the time, drying it for hours? And check out your fingernails, covered with pink. Is that a blank page? Is that minimalism? Is that less?*

Sylvia looked at her fingernails, which glittered with pink. *Cut, cut, C-U-T!!!*

Her inner voice was on a roll.

STOP! she pleaded.

No response. Smart devil. The inner voice knew when to stop.

She begged for tears, hoping for relief, like vomiting when nauseous. She pictured a pencil changing rapidly from fat to thin, from yellow to green to transparent outlined in purple, flipping upside down and back again, dancing all alone, its eraser sensuously wet with saliva, its point sharp and deadly. She saw fingers with pink nails holding the pencil. Paper appeared beneath the point and the pencil began to write. *CUT! JUST DO IT!* And then everything melted from view, except pink against a black background.

Sylvia cut: her hair, her fingernails, even her fingertips.

A pale, thin, sad young woman with short red hair and stubby, flesh colored fingernails walked into the office the next day. Blood and new scabs marked her fingertips.

"Sylvia? I can hardly recognize you," said Sally. "What happened? Where's your gorgeous hair? Your nails?"

"Yeah. I just cut stuff off. Needed to. It's about time."

You pathetic thing. You look like crap. Maybe you ought to cut off a few fingers, or an ear — maybe your tongue and be done with it. Make me your only voice.

Her inner voice had a victorious, relentless quality.

"You should go home and rest," Sally suggested, looking worried. "We have a light load of submissions this week. Here's a couple of pieces you might look through at home if you feel like it. This one's a coincidence; it sounds right up your alley. It's called 'Less is not Enough' and, believe it or not, it's by a Michael Slender, your namesake. Ever hear of the guy?"

Sylvia's knees buckled, blood drained from her face.

"Sylvia? Can you hear me? Do you know him?"

She heard Sally's words as if they came from another source, like she was drifting under anesthesia.

"Sorry...yes, I hear you...don't feel well today...maybe I'm getting sick... no, no, don't know the guy...Michael Slender you say? Funny...maybe it's a pseudonym...yes, okay, I'll read the story...see you tomorrow...bye.

Her hand shook as she held the first page of her father's short story. She recognized his abbreviated writing style, which was similar to her own: no bullshit, minimalist, surgical. The story, submitted as fiction, was about a rich man, Frank, plagued with social guilt for having more than he needs. He lived alone, drifted from job to job, and felt worthless. He started giving to charity, and as his wealth decreased, his spirits rose. Soon he had little money left and needed a job. He worked his way up to maitred' of a classy restaurant, married, had twin girls...

Twin girls!! My god, it's amazing, like my dream, the one I didn't write about, said her inner voice, now a friend, a confidant, feeling disoriented.

...named Sophia and Laurel, who he loved. They were beautiful redheads, small priceless gems, the glitter in his life. Sophia was sweet, smart and modest; Laurel cunning, aggressive and ruthless. He devoted his attention to Laurel because she demanded it, and made do with silly jokes with Sophia, who always sparkled as if she were happy.

Had enough, baby doll. Can you take all this?

She bit her lower lip and continued.

Frank went to a conference, met a sleazy woman, divorced his wife, moved to a Caribbean island, lost contact with his family and died of AIDS.

The story was mundane, disappointing. Sylvia turned the page and read the short epilogue:

"In his final days, Frank ambled aimlessly in his home. His wife left him, but he didn't care. With the shadow of death hanging over him, and hurting from deep sorrow for the life choices he had made, he composed a letter to his sweet daughter, Sophia.

Your gentle spirit is the love of my life. I think of you daily, your green eyes sparkling, your red hair on fire. I saw your heart aching, and I didn't reach out to you. I didn't know how. I still don't, but I love you as much as I know how to love, more than I ever loved anybody or anything in my life. I know it was not enough. If I learned anything, it's that less is not enough. If I could do it over again, I would. I'm sorry."

I'm speechless, said her inner voice.

Me too, she answered aloud.

She closed her eyes waiting to hear more from her inner voice, or to see a pencil playing games with written words. But instead, she felt a trickle of wetness running down her cheeks. Tears, sweet tears.

It's okay, baby doll, really, go ahead.

Her inner voice retreated, as if hiding in her soul. Nothing seemed to matter anymore, because the fight seemed finished.

She cried.

"You're looking better today, Sylvia," said Sally. "But I prefer you with long hair."

"Me too. I'll let it grow again. And put green polish on my nails, to match my eyes."

"Did you get a chance to read the story I gave you yesterday?"

"Yes."

"What did you think?" Sally asked.

"It has lots of things that people care about today: divorce, loss, AIDS…and I liked the epilogue. Touching. But, I don't know…no, yes, yes…I think it might be published. Let me know what you think."

"Okay. I'll read it and, assuming I like it, you can work with him."

"I'd rather not; you do it. Yeah, please, you handle it. Okay?"

"Sure."

Sylvia whistled as she bounced into her office.

Right on, baby doll. Right ON.

The Ugly President

Twenty years ago, President Filene Debaluchie Starenovsky died as she reigned – with grace. A month after her memorial service, a publishing house asked me to write a book about her unorthodox rise to prominence. Accepting the offer would have crowned my career as a political scientist and her campaign manager, and yet I refused. It would have been impossible for me to be objective.

Now, an old man of 87 who never married, I still think about Filene as if I were writing the book I never did. I confess that I loved her, but I kept it secret. If only she hadn't been so ugly: a thick neck, pockmarked face, sunken cheekbones, disproportionately small nose, and thin hirsute upper lip that some ridiculed as sprinkled with poppy seeds. Her enlarged chin glowed with a yellow-orange patina resembling ancient walrus ivory. Deep crevices lined her wide forehead. A mild case of hemi-facial spasm was often mistaken for a neurotic tick, but there was nothing neurotic about Filene. She was a short (four foot eleven in bare feet), well-adjusted bundle of positive energy, and brilliant.

Beneath Filene's deformities, I saw a mysterious and beautiful woman. Thick bifocals covered blue-green iris whirlpools surrounding dense black pupils. Idealistic dreams spilled out of her eyes. I wished I could have slid down those dark tunnels of her pupils into her mind. However, I lacked the courage to court Filene. I remember when Filene and I had dinner together to celebrate her passing the bar examination. She was beaming and looked at me in a special way that night, wanting more than friendship. But I didn't respond. After dinner I drove her home, said good night and congratulations, and we went our separate ways. I think it would have been very different if she were pretty.

But being ugly didn't hinder Filene's spirit and unique career in politics. Her courage was greater than my cowardice.

One Tuesday in 2036, a presidential election year, Filene went to her law office, as usual, wearing a cream-colored blouse covered with multicolored stitched emblems of diving women that she'd bought when she attended the Olympic games years earlier. That shirt was her good luck charm. It had a worn, yellowish edge around the neckline from extensive wear and was tight around her waist, revealing the effect of innumerable doughnuts she had devoured over the years (she had a serious sweet tooth). That day Filene had decided, incredibly, to test the frightening world of politics. When she astonished her clients that she was suspending her practice in order to run for President of the United States, Sarah Jones, who was in the midst of a divorce, cried in despair.

"That's terrible," Sarah said. "I'll lose everything to my ugly bastard husband."

"Nonsense, Sarah," Filene answered in a mucous-laden rattle from years of smoking cigarillos (a nasty habit she refused to quit). "You don't know the first thing about ugly. While I'm not able to help you right now, maybe I can help a whole lot of other people in the future."

On her final day of practicing law, Filene retrieved her titanium crutch, which stabilized her tilt to the left due to a congenitally shorter left leg. She took one last look at the Picasso print of Don Quixote (her hero) on the office wall and sighed. On her way out, she glanced at her reflection in the mirror by the door, recoiled and smashed it with her crutch. She had told me that if her clients didn't spend so much time looking at their pretty selves they might be more compassionate towards others. I had no idea how significant that was at the time, and felt a pang of guilt for having often inspected myself when I entered and left her office.

Filene came directly to my house after work the day she'd decided to enter politics at the national level. She said, "I don't want to just putter around at the local level." She was exuberant. Filene always thought big.

The problem started when she had railed with relentless passion against the maddeningly conservative federal government one evening when she was having dinner at my apartment with a few of my politically involved friends. In jest, although regretting immediately the teasing, I told Filene, "If you didn't lean so much to the left you wouldn't need a crutch. Why don't you put your money where your mouth is and run for President?"

Completely unexpectedly, absurdly so, Filene became obsessed with the challenge.

I took the bait and began to encourage her to run for President in earnest, and even tested the waters by campaigning for her in any way I could. I talked her up to friends, students and acquaintances. I convinced Jamie Sikes, a young representative, to advance her candidacy. To my surprise – bewilderment – and Filene's delight, the buzz about Filene took off like a forest fire on a dry, windy day. Her entrance into the race for president was political satire – an entertaining reality show. Few gave her any chance, and it was unsettling to me. I knew how sincere Filene was, how driven to succeed and to show people that there was a beautiful, significant person within her unfortunate body. I was scared for her.

Filene's political efforts would not have been possible if not for the decadent state of the country. Apart from a plunging economy, racism lurked in the shadows, and terrorism that had metastasized from ISIS had not been contained. The media manipulated public opinions with questionable polls. The newly appointed Board of Aspirations and Moral Supremacy (BAMS), comprising mainly clergy and right-wing politicians, was gaining traction. Ladders made the fifteen-foot high concrete wall built along the northern and southern borders of the country to prevent illegal immigration porous. The country was in the doldrums.

Despite the bleakness of the times, or maybe because of it, Filene argued enthusiastically that she was a viable candidate for President. She insisted that her success as a lawyer would substitute for her lack of political experience, since one of the major problems was poor law enforcement. What confidence she had, despite the odds against her, and what arrogance as well to feel entitled. But that was Filene, a spectrum of personalities in one amazingly ugly package.

My involvement came when she said, "Jake, please help me. I need my Sancho Panza." Sancho Panza, the sidekick, the down-to-earth foil for Don Quixote's heroics. Her plea aroused a sense of *déjà vu* stemming from when I supported her enthusiastically for high school student body president. Remembering my heartbreak and her despondency at her landslide loss to the football quarterback gave me pause about replaying the old days at the national level, but her eyes sparkled, as they so often did when she was inspired, that I was ready to do anything for her. She recognized my vulnerability. I was putty in her hands.

"Okay, Filene," I said, flattered. "What do you want me to do? Be your campaign manager?"

She lit up. "Oh, thank you! Thank you!"

I was taken aback by her animated gratitude, but the need to project an attractive image for such a physically ugly candidate seemed as impossible as painting a colorful picture with a severely limited palette.

She read my doubts (I was always impressed at her ability to sense what I was thinking) and volunteered, "Never mind, Jake. The future is like the proverbial black box. Let's take a chance!"

And so we embarked on an historic journey.

Filene gained financial backing, ironically, from a Superpac of cosmetic companies. She spoke tirelessly around the country, and pulled upset after upset in the primaries. When asked why she believed herself qualified to be President, she used her lack of national political experience as a badge of honesty. She also stressed she had no political dues to pay. Full acceptance of her candidacy came when she compared her situation to the success of Donald Trump twenty years earlier.

"Not everything can be explained," she said. "Sometimes things are just the way they are."

She spoke freely of her unattractive appearance, saying that it was no fault of her own, and stressed that it sensitized her to the unfairness of life, a sentiment always received with agreeing nods. She repeated, "Would anyone with my looks even try to cast a false image, or be able to succeed in doing so?" Media pundits loved her because she was so ugly, which attracted huge audiences. The necessity for political change drew many opportunistic hopefuls to challenge her, but one by one they withdrew, not up to Filene's spunk, making her appear as a formidable winner. A lucky scandal involving one of Filene's main opponents in a prostitution scam using undocumented workers obliterated him from contention like lightening striking a dead tree. Filene became the sober dark horse, the potential for positive change, she had predicted.

There was also the comical element. I would have dwelled on this bittersweet aspect of her nomination as a metaphor for decay in the country if I had written my book. If viewed as a clown, Filene was a tragic figure, not funny, but a "little tramp" of humanity who did for politics what Charlie Chaplin did for movies. Her subtle use of humor was brilliant and effective, and instead of a scapegoat, she was seen as a savior. However, even when the political winds favored ugly Filene, it still seemed incredible that she would be actually nominated. Neither the pundits nor voters truly believed she could win the general election.

But she won the needed number of delegates and was nominated to represent her party. When interviewed after the convention, she said in a deadpan voice, "I won because of my charm." Everyone laughed. One insensitive editorialist concluded that, "Pretty doesn't work anymore. It's time to try ugly!"

Americans settled down to the business of choosing between Filene and her opponent – a good-looking, broad-smiling two-term Senator from Wyoming named James Thornton – in the general election. Six-foot three and silver-tongued, Thornton commanded an impressive presence, especially next to tiny Filene. She looked like a squashed rodent next to a Greek God. Since Thornton's striking image carried weight, as powerful images do, he jumped to a lop-sided two-digit lead in the polls. Just three weeks before the election, people had given up on Filene and prepared to watch the final debate with the macabre fascination of seeing blood spurting from a deep gash.

I was struck by how calm Filene was the day before the Great Debate. I capitalize Great Debate because it was just that, a great debate that will still be studied generations from now.

At first I mistook Filene's quiet demeanor before the event for resignation. All I could do was put my hand on her shoulder (I rarely touched her) and say, "I'm so proud of what you've done, Filene." She responded with a half-smile directed inwards, as if I weren't even there. Although this made me feel sadly excluded, for some reason it also gave me hope that she might have found a way to accept defeat graciously.

Thornton came to the debate bloated with confidence in a dark suit and red tie with his lovely second wife twenty years his junior (the former Miss Idaho) cradling an infant. Two spotless teen-age children from his first wife and an assortment of relatives also accompanied him. He chatted casually with his adoring public and uttered condescending banalities as, "I'm proud to debate the distinguished and learned Ms. Starenovsky," and "It's an honor for me be on the same stage as my worthy opponent."

Filene wore her lucky Olympic blouse with the embroidered diving women. I was her only 'family' and stayed in the background. She spoke to no one before the debate and hobbled to her podium as a solitary, battle-scarred warrior nourished entirely from within. I had no idea that she was preparing to do something enormous.

The debate started at 9 p.m. sharp, and was recorded verbatim. I would have reproduced it word for word in my book, but here I limit my comments to what I consider the highlights. Just thinking about this moment in history gives me shivers.

The moderator began by addressing the sorrowful state of the nation. "People are suffering both economically and emotionally. They have lost confidence in our great country and worry about its future. I ask each of you to state how, if elected President, you would elevate the spirit of our citizens. First, Senator Thornton."

The Senator expanded his raised chest Pilates style. He lifted weights daily and jogged twice a week. It showed.

Thornton said in a resonating voice, "If elected President I will emphasize our need to maintain the moral courage and faith to obey God's will. God is just, and we will prevail at His discretion. I will set the tone for our souls to converse with our inner sense of what is right. I would say let the dialogue begin. We all know right from wrong and good from bad. God will bless our democracy. My administration will be marked by the golden rule: Do unto others, as you would have others do unto you. I will be the balm that soothes and ultimately heals our wounds. That's what compassionate Presidents do."

After his response, Thornton gazed above the audience projecting the humility of self-righteousness. He had acted the role of a benevolent minister once in his earlier movie career, earning him the nickname 'Reverend'.

Filene slouched as she clung to the shortened podium with her right hand, her left armpit propped up by her titanium crutch. She refused to sit despite the difficulty of standing for the duration of the debate. She knew that she must act like a man.

"Yes, indeed," muttered Filene half-heartedly but loud enough to be heard.

"How so, Ms. Starenovsky?" asked the Senator. "Do you agree with me?"

The moderator interrupted. "Please, confine your comments to answering *my* questions. It is your turn now, Ms. Starenovsky. How would you reverse the state of the union if elected President?"

Filene spoke without notes because she could not trust that her hemi-facial spasm would allow her to keep her right eye open enough to read fluently under the stressful conditions of the debate.

"I agree with Senator Thornton when he says to be kind to one another. But, with my looks – goodness, how shall I put it? – I think I can speak with more authority than the Senator on being kind or thoughtful." She sighed, and then squinted as if to tighten her resolve.

I couldn't imagine what she had in mind and leaned forward to hear what she was going to say next. The audience looked confused as well; a few laughed under their breath, transforming a solemn occasion into black humor. If people came for a circus, they probably believed they were being treated to exactly that: a straight-faced clown sparring with a pompous buffoon.

The moderator interrupted the snickers. "We seem to be drifting, Ms. Starenovsky. Please elaborate on how your 'looks', as you put it, gives you more authority on how to behave or be more compassionate than Senator Thornton?"

"Very well. I had to learn to be considerate to myself, not just to others. What can be more difficult than that? My parents were beautiful people, bless their hearts, and they had mirrors in every room. They loved looking at themselves. They were lovely. But when I saw myself in the mirror as a little girl, it wasn't possible to…to avoid revulsion. All those mirrors. *Reflecting monsters*, I called them."

She paused to let her comments sink in, and a heavy quiet settled like a thick mist. There were no more snickers. My palms were sweating.

Filene continued. "I became irritable and envious and unhappy. How can one look ugly and feel beautiful? The Senator suggests that we adopt a policy of doing unto others, as we would like others to do unto us. A noble sentiment, but it's not easy for blessed, beautiful people like all of you in this great country, like Senator Thornton, to understand what that means to someone like me. Would I want others to pretend to ignore my appearance, like beautiful people might think is the right thing to do? Or, would I want them to lie and say I look pretty? Oh my, Senator, ladies and gentlemen, being ugly is no bargain, and…I'm ugly, let's face it, as is the state of our nation. I have a unique perspective of the difficulty of doing unto others what I would want them to do unto me. The *image* of being kind has nothing to do with being kind. One must look deeper."

She paused again. "Excuse me," she said, and then blew her nose into a wrinkled Kleenex. "That's better."

I was uncertain whether Filene was holding back tears at this point in the debate.

Filene's comments created an awkward moment. Thornton shifted his weight from one foot to the other, back and forth. One could sense that the stupefied audience was developing a new respect and sympathy for her. I was impressed at her honesty, admiring her as always, and proud to be her campaign manager. I became cautiously hopeful she would escape this debate intact. The moderator rubbed his jaw and removed his glasses, pretending wisdom. This was more than an unusual debate; it was one for all times.

"How did you 'look deeper', Ms. Starenovsky?" asked the moderator.

"Oh yes, what did I do? I eliminated every monstrous mirror from our house. I pulverized the mirrors in fact, and sucked up the broken glass with a vacuum cleaner, leaving not a trace. My parents were angry at first, but they understood.

"I was exhilarated. No more being defined by my image! I decided never to look at myself again. Unfortunately I broke that vow when I left my office to run for the presidency, but then I smashed that mirror too. I was no longer the most important person on earth or a prisoner of my reflected image. No more arguments between my invisible soul and my too visible self. It was quite amazing. The opaque wall hiding the world became transparent. We value freedom above all else, but never consider that we are bound by our own image. When I discarded mirrors I felt free for the first time in my life. Free from myself. And what happened to me? Did I get prettier? I can't answer that because I didn't look at myself anymore, but I doubt it. It didn't matter."

"What did matter?" asked the moderator.

"Yes, what did matter?" echoed Senator Thornton.

Chatter rippled through the audience.

"I was what mattered, not my image. As President, I would be honest as to who we are as a nation. We shouldn't rely on God to save us. We must save ourselves."

Filene was on a roll. She was so excited and expressive that I can't remember if I have her words exactly correct. But it doesn't matter. Her enthusiasm and honesty were infectious. Her spirit hovered above her tiny, deformed body, above the moderator and James Thornton, above all of us. The spectators turned to their neighbors, gesticulating and whispering to each other, taken completely by surprise.

The moderator tried to restore order. "Quiet, please!" he shouted.

Senator Thornton spoke up as the moderator looked on. "Well…um…we need to let the voters decide whether the absence of image will substitute for the presence of God."

I was overjoyed in a way that I could never have expressed in a book; it was not political or strategic. It was guttural. If Thornton realized that he was in trouble after Filene's emotional and honest disclosure, he never showed it. He just smiled and puffed his chest. The debate continued.

"Senator Thornton," asked the moderator, "what would you do about our deteriorating image abroad?"

"Deteriorating image abroad?" repeated the Senator. "I don't know what you mean. We are spreading democracy to a grateful world and everybody wants to come here. Look how many illegal aliens scale our protective wall at night to gain entrance. They love us!"

"Ms. Starenovsky, do you have a response?"

"I certainly do," she said. "The Senator has put his finger precisely on the problem by accident. People are deceived by the images of our promises, and we let them down. Images again. Ban them, I say.

"Look, there are so many examples from our daily life. Think about our image that thin is beautiful? The result is many miserable, well-fed people amid a growing population of walking skin and bones." Filene patted her bulging sides and everyone laughed. "Let's throw away faulty images and be honest. People eat, and good food makes them happy and secure. A little fat is okay. Let's not continue to stress the false shadow of beauty. I repeat: ban the image; promote the truth!"

I found Filene's sympathetic thoughts on weight extraordinary, especially with so many overweight voters in the country.

A few moments later, Thornton went on the offensive and said, "I think Ms. Starenovsky is being double-faced. Why…"

Before he could even ask his question Filene interrupted sharply with a question of her own. "Why, Senator, would I wear this face I have if I had another?"

Applause erupted.

"Quiet!!" blurted the exasperated moderator.

The spectators marveled at Filene's demolishment of James Thornton, but I suddenly felt sorry for him. All his efforts and sincere beliefs had turned to mud, and while Filene never gloated, I knew her well enough to recognize a shade of triumph that so often hides beneath a thin coat of modesty.

Senator Thornton made a last attempt to salvage the situation. "Might it not, Ms. Starenovsky, be the ultimate honesty to see ourselves in one of these 'reflective monsters' as others see us? Wouldn't that help us improve our image abroad and heal our wounds at home?"

I was taken aback with the implications and intelligence of this question. I no longer knew image from substance.

"Ms. Starenovsky? Do you have a final response to the Senator's question?" asked the moderator.

Filene fiddled with her crutch and allowed a few seconds to expand into the illusion of wisdom. Then, in a quiet voice, yet sufficient to be heard by everyone, she said, "An image will always be just an image."

The audience scrunched their brows knowingly and nodded in unison.

Senator Thornton's broad shoulders sagged.

Filene had turned the election around in her favor. But I knew this was not enough. She needed a catchy slogan encompassing a simple idea that voters could relate to. I didn't know exactly what to use for Filene's campaign slogan. 'End Images' didn't have sufficient punch; it was too abstract. Then, a morbid opportunity struck.

Just next to Filene's Chicago campaign headquarters, construction workers dropped a large wall mirror from the thirteenth floor of a building being renovated. The mirror fell on four teenagers walking in the street and killed one of them instantly. The two headlines: "Dropped Mirror Kills Innocent Victims" and "FDS Pledges Ban on Images," were reported sequentially on national news broadcasts. The headlines apparently fused in voters' minds, and Filene's repudiation of mirrors and images grew into public opinion. Imagine that! I guess there are some things that you can't direct or predict. They just happen. Following the mirror incident, Filene's public appearances started and ended with everyone chanting in unison, "…No More Mirrors…No More Mirrors…"

Mirrors became the reflecting monsters of images and death.

Mirror sales fell, moods soared and everyone became more polite, less stingy with compliments or with acknowledgements of achievements of others and above all, more compassionate and empathic, all consistent with Filene's ideas. Even I stopped wasting energy worrying about how I appeared and focused on how I saw others. If I had done this earlier, who knows, I may have courted Filene. It was as if she had turned inside out; her character became her appearance.

News anchors paid less attention to appearance and entertainment, and their reports became more substantive and objective. Underdogs gained self-respect, the severely ill hoped for miracle cures, and the miserable majority of neglected people glowed with empowerment. A great equalization had occurred. The euphoria translated into votes resulting in a landslide victory for Filene. For that brief interval of time no one considered her ugly. By banning mirrors, images lost their phantom weight and floated away as imaginary ghosts. An influential columnist wrote perceptively, "Filene's genius was to eliminate images altogether rather than try to alter them."

James Thornton conceded two hours after the polls closed and graciously said, "Congratulations, and may God help us."

Filene continued to promote the elimination of mirrors as a metaphor of her administration. She was strict on false advertising, spoke honestly of the country's deficiencies, and embraced the qualities of foreign countries when it was justified. She worked well with Congress, the economy stabilized and morale lifted. The first six months of her administration remain as a solitary, peaceful jewel of history.

Then tragedy struck. At 6:23 a.m. on the first Wednesday of June 2037, several members of the staff heard a thud in her bedroom. They rushed into the chamber and found Filene collapsed on the floor quivering with spasms. She had tried to go to the bathroom and suffered a stroke. A staff member called me immediately. I lived close by, and when I arrived, Filene was resting in her bed as the White House doctor examined her.

She whispered, "My end has come. I'm sorry to leave you all with my rotting flesh." She continued, looking embarrassed. "I have a last request, if you don't mind. I would like to see myself once more before I become invisible forever. Could you... bring me...a *mirror?*"

What an astonishing, disorienting request! I thought about the complex, contradictory layers of motivation. Was James Thornton correct in saying that Filene was double-faced? How many faces do any of us have? Are image and substance just two sides of the same coin, inseparable, one impossible without the other? Three staff members dashed out of the bedroom. Each returned with a mirror they had been hiding – hiding! They looked at one another with chagrin. They held the 'reflective monsters' in a row before Filene since she was too weak to hold one herself.

Filene looked startled when she saw her image. The mirrors were unintentionally tilted such that when she peered into one she saw a row of her images. She looked at me imploringly and asked meekly, "Which one am I?"

"All of them?" I said, unsure of myself.

"Perhaps," she answered, looking into my eyes. "How remarkable that, as I am dying, these mirrors recreate my image over and over again. And how strange," she went on, "that if a bullet would strike the mirror before me, this one, the one I am looking at directly…" and she reached out with difficulty and touched her glass face, "…it would shatter just the mirror it hits, but from my perspective it would also destroy my images in the other mirrors, without affecting me physically." After a heartbreaking pause, she said, "Oh, such nonsense…"

"No, not nonsense," I assured her.

For the first time I saw Filene as a spectrum of conflated, blurred mirages that I should have been trying to separate from one another using a prism, not a mirror, buried within my mind. Which Filene had conquered me and moved everyone else – the idealist, the superior underdog, the modest warrior, the victorious politician, the thoughtful activist, the ambitious, peaceful, humorous, sad, ugly, dying woman before me? There were even more Filenes, all real. Of course I couldn't have written that book. I would have needed to write a series of voluminous books using reflecting paper and invisible ink. I'm glad I never tried. Angels, like spirits, must be felt; they cannot be understood.

Filene was mourned by people throughout the world and considered a saint of sorts, as much as a political leader can be. The vice president served out the term, and then senator Thornton was elected president on the platform that God is merciful. Wars resumed, self-serving attitudes blossomed, and the world was back to normal.

Except for me. I was a changed person. When Filene closed her eyes for the last time, I felt great sadness and regret, but also a tinge of relief. When her spasms ceased and her contorted face looked content, striking in fact, I found her more beautiful than

I ever considered myself handsome, and was humbled. The deep creases in her forehead had transformed into narrow, tranquil streams flowing nowhere in particular. From her mysterious aura, as might have come from her hero, Don Quixote in glorious armor, I gained a new understanding of loneliness, both from her perspective and from mine, and felt privileged.

The Optimist

Mr. Mellows squirms his 6-foot-five inch hulk onto a flimsy wooden chair. The low tabletop presses down on his knees. A bare 40-watt fluorescent light in the center of the ceiling flickers from the ceiling in the barren room; brown stains mar the blond, dusty hardwood floor. The gray paint on the walls is peeling. A cockroach lies belly-up near the warped door with an empty hole where the doorknob used to be. A dark cloud eclipses the sun, sharpening the relief of the crack in the glass pane of the curtainless window.

In a print framed in cracked plastic hung crooked on the wall, a lovely young woman wearing a straw hat with a pink ribbon milks a Jersey cow in a barn surrounded by aspens bearing golden autumn leaves. Rocks faintly veined with reds and copper-greens protrude from a creek that runs out of the picture and away.

An ambitious young reporter from the Front Royal Magazine sits across from Mr. Mellows. He centers his horn-rimmed glasses against the ridge of his nose and reviews his notes. It has taken him almost a year to arrange this interview, with *the* Mr. Mellows of United Steel Corporation. He hopes a successful interview will improve his chances of being selected for a community events reporter position advertised by the Potomac Gazette – a more illustrious publication.

Mr. Mellows scans the room dispassionately, scratches the side of his neck and runs his fingers through his thinning hair. When his eyes lock on the farm girl gripping the udders, he sighs.

"Makes me envious," he says, sweating in the July humidity of Washington.

"What's that?"

"The picture. Is that the life, or what? A sweet girl, countryside, nature."

"Yes, sir. Know what you mean. Let's get to work."

The interviewer appears nervous as he reads his prepared first question.

"Mr. Mellows isn't your real name, is it? What is your birth name?"

"That's irrelevant, isn't it?" answers Mr. Mellows, insensitive to the interviewer's youth. "I answer to Mr. Mellows. I made Mr. Mellows who he is."

The interviewer searches for a response.

"But, sir, people want to know more about you. You're a mystery. Nobody even knows your first name."

"First name, last name, middle initial. Big deal."

Appearing slightly flustered, the interviewer presses on.

"My name is Bob," he says.

"Just Bob?" Mr. Mellow asks.

"Ringling. Bob Ringling."

"Related to the circus family?"

"Not really. Everybody asks me that. Gets annoying."

"See what I mean? Why don't you call yourself Bob Circling, eliminate the annoyance, Start anew. Pick your own name."

The interviewer scratches his chin. "I thought I was interviewing you."

"Yes, correct. But I'm not sure why. What have I done that's worth an interview?" Mr. Mellows asks with false modesty.

The interviewer shakes his head. "You're on TV, on billboards; there's even talk of you being selected by *Time Magazine* as the Man of the Year."

"Ridiculous. I'll never beat out Mayor Gargani. Do you know that his wife's a Rockefeller?"

The interviewer ignores the question and looks at the second question on his list. "The rumor is that your parents emigrated from Europe just before World War II. Is that true?"

"Excuse me for switching the subject, but why is everything so run down here? The place looks like a war zone."

The interviewer clenches his jaw.

"You asked for a neutral site without publicity. You didn't want me to come to your house or office or to meet me at a restaurant. A commercial real estate agent let me use this place he's selling. I know it's a dump, but it's the best I could do."

"I like it," responds Mr. Mellows, who finally reveals that he's capable of smiling. He looks at the farm girl in the print. The interviewer follows his gaze.

"About your parents," he says, trying to refocus the interview. "Were they business people?"

He is no longer looking at his notes.

"Heavens no! My father was a molecular biologist, may he rest in peace, and my mother worked for a tree company."

"A tree company?"

Mr. Mellows thinks a moment. "Yeah. She was tiny, only 4 foot 7, and loved to climb trees, heaven knows why. She didn't weigh enough to break the small branches so she was able to get to places that are hard to trim. Most of her work was on the estates of rich guys."

"Pretty dangerous. Did it influence you to take risks like you've done in your work?"

"You bet, except that she fell off a tulip poplar by a tennis court on her fortieth birthday and bye-bye. I was twelve. That made me the only child of a single parent. My dad told me to get used to it; nothing lasts forever. You might write that down. He was tough."

"Wow! Quite an experience for a 12 year-old."

The interviewer scribbles *'nothing lasts forever, tough father'* on his pad.

Mr. Mellows puts his left hand in the pocket of his gray cotton pants; coins jingle. He loosens his maroon tie and undoes the top button of his shirt, crisp white except for the symmetrical grey discolorations under his armpits.

The interviewer wipes his brow. "Your father must have been a big man to have a tiny wife and a son like you. You're… well…huge."

"Not really. He was about 5 foot 10 at a stretch. Don't *ever* try to psyche out nature. It'll fool you every time. Nothing's predictable. That's been a guiding principle of mine. You can write that down too."

"Yes, sir."

The interviewer writes on his notepad *'nothing's predictable, guiding…'* He stops writing before finishing and looks lost in thought.

"Hello?" says Mr. Mellows.

"Sorry."

The interviewer asks another question.

"Was your father a well-known scientist? That is, were you exposed to fame as a youngster?"

"Hardly, although it depends on what you call fame. Most of the people in his building at work knew him, as did a dozen or so scientists around the world. He got an award once, from a pharmaceutical company. No, it was from an entomology society. He was far out. Studied sticky stuff on the bottoms of the feet of certain kinds of bugs. I forget their scientific name. Busted his ass and sweated every little detail of his work, and nobody cared, except those few peers. They argued like crazy as to who discovered what first. Man, it would make a boring movie. Watching him taught me a lot about life, even though it sort of broke my heart."

Mr. Mellows hesitates. "Science is fascinating though. Something about it that's…well…that rings true…" He looks sad and then adds, "Science doesn't depend on perception to be right."

"Is that what you learned from your father?"

Mr. Mellows checks his gold Rolex and then stares at the picture on the wall.

"Mr. Mellows, what did you learn from your father?"

"Yes, yes. Excuse me. She's so pretty. I mean, *really* charming. Like the girl with a pearl earring by Vermeer. Know that painting?"

"Yes, sir." The interviewer looks at the picture and then he returns to his question.

"About what you learned from your father. What was it?"

"Give awards, don't get them. The percentage is much higher, and everybody else waits on the edge of their chair rather than you. Makes you far more important, and you don't have to say thank you or grovel explaining how you don't deserve it, that it's all due to others, and…well."

The interviewer scribbles some notes, underlines a phrase.

"Mr. Mellows, how did you make USC so financially successful and innovative? The use of large sheets of pliable, green steel that's comfortable to walk on, like grass, and generate energy from soil heat. That was brilliant! How did that come about?"

Mr. Mellows stands up and paces the room. He sneaks a look at the farm girl again, whispers inaudibly to himself and turns to the interviewer.

"The first thing I did when I took over the company is strip titles from everyone. Hierarchy stifles creativity. It helped morale and ideas flowed like water. A green, soft, energy-producing woven steel grass substitute was just one of the ideas, and it came from a new recruit. Young people are too foolish to be cautious. They take chances. You're young. You know what I mean. Do you take chances?"

The interviewer blushes and doesn't answer. He asks, "Didn't that create insecurity for the senior people?"

"Are you kidding? Equality is a great thing. It gives everyone the same opportunity."

When the interviewer hears "equality" and "opportunity" his eyes shine.

Mr. Mellows continues. "Everybody wins. I coordinated the show, like a...a....manager of a baseball team. Yes, that's it. All baseball players in the major leagues are great athletes. So why does one team do better than another? The manager, of course. He decides who does what, when, why. He's the person who deserves the credit. That's why managers are always getting fired if their team doesn't win. The owners know that a different manager may make them winners. What an inspiration, a great manager! You can write *that* down in your notes. 'Management is art'. Yes sir," beams Mr. Mellows.

The interviewer writes on his pad *'management is art'*. He also adds some comments to himself in messy handwriting with a disapproving expression on his face.

Mr. Mellows walks to the picture and closes the fingers of his left hand around an imaginary udder. The interviewer watches.

"It would be an inspiration to…*younger people*…to hear how you began such a successful career," says the interviewer.

Mr. Mellows gazes at the floor.

"My path to success? I never did or said anything that the majority didn't agree with. Then I implemented it. No need to be a 'lab hermit' doing stuff that no one cares about. I never believed in originality by obscurity. It's reverse snobbism. Listen to the voices out there. It's like my garbage company."

"Garbage company, Mr. Mellows?"

"Yes! It was a hoot."

"A hoot? Garbage?"

Mr. Mellows ambles back to the picture, rubs his index finger along the top of the frame and winks at the farm girl.

The interviewer looks annoyed.

"Oh, it's kind of silly, really. I was just out of college. Let's see: that was just over forty years ago. The local government wanted to put a county dump in a large field in a posh neighborhood. They said everyone needed to pay their dues. They called it a landfill. Land filled with crap and germs and ugliness is what they meant. I hate euphemisms, don't you?"

"I guess so."

"Well, when I read about that in the papers, you know, when newspapers were still in hardcopies, I convinced several families in the neighborhood to start a garbage business, to take advantage of the situation rather than whine about it. I told them they could make money living next to a landfill by picking up trash and dumping it across the street. It would be a local convenience. One fellow had a wooded lot that was just… *there*…doing nothing but looking pretty…so I convinced him to make it a parking lot for our garbage trucks, which would be camouflaged by trees. I got some investors to go along with the idea and arranged the zoning by calling my business 'estate purification assistance'."

Mr. Mellows winks at the interviewer, then says in a low voice implying complicity, "The local government interpreted 'purified estates' as more valuable than 'unpurified estates', know what I mean? 'Purified estates' translated to higher taxes, so they had no problem giving us the proper zoning. I guess I don't hate euphemisms after all." He pauses. "I disbanded the business after a couple of years although it made money."

He rubs his right thumb and index finger together indicating it made a lot of money.

"Some people may knock the green stuff, aspire to higher ideals, like poetry or how bugs walk on the ceiling, whatever. Without money...well, nothing's done and people starve. You might want to write that down too. Money counts."

"I guess," says the interviewer. He writes *'money counts'* and follows it with two question marks. He looks at the flickering fluorescent light as if it bothers him.

"Well, young man, it isn't easy, is it? The idea of interviewing me was more appealing than actually doing it. Right? Am I correct?"

The interviewer focuses on the tabletop like a little boy being reprimanded. "No, sir, it's not so easy. You're not helping. I mean. Your life is...*interesting*."

"Sure is."

"*Amazing* is more like it. You make things work, you twist and turn, and there you are at the finish line, smiling and alone. But...who are you, really?"

A siren screams in the street. Mr. Mellows walks to the window and looks below. He sees mid-day traffic, a few pedestrians, some trash on the sidewalk, a leashed dog pissing against the lamppost while its owner, a middle-aged Chinese woman, looks the other way. Mr. Mellow turns to the interviewer. He straightens with resolve, ignores the radiating nerve pain down his right leg due to spinal stenosis, returns briskly to the table and sits down.

"Let's go on. I promised you an interview and an interview is what you will get. Who am I? I told you. I am Mr. Mellows, a self-made man with a self-made name. I carved my way through life, like a sculptor. You see? Do you understand? Each time a chess piece moves, the game has a new structure, the opportunities are not the same. I am the chessboard. The pieces are my life. I am both sides of the game, black and white, and when one game is over, another starts and I am still there. The game cannot be played without me. Without the chessboard the pieces would have no place to move. Without land, architects couldn't build houses, without air, pilots couldn't fly planes, without nature, scientists couldn't discover anything. The medium is everything. Do you understand that?"

"No, sir, not really."

Mr. Mellow looks at the fluffy clouds above the aspens in the picture.

The interviewer writes '*chessboard, medium is everything*'.

"After the garbage, I mean 'estate purification' business, I was asked to be an advisor for the state government on urban planning. I thought it strange since I had no credentials in that area, but they told me the concept of merging sanitary engineering, as they called my garbage business, with the suburbs was brilliant. Before I knew it I was on the zoning commission, planning changes in traffic patterns, designing recreational facilities at the junctions between urban and suburban areas, joining different lifestyles as it were, and so on and so forth. I was given a green medal when I decided to leave after a couple of years."

"Why green? Do you mean for energy conservation?"

"Maybe. The bronze part dangled from green cloth."

"What did you do then?"

"Good question. I always had a weak spot for science, I guess because of my father, but mainly I saw it as another way to make a buck. I figured I could get support for anything scientific if people thought they would benefit from the results. They forget about the gap between the science and the reality of having it be useful."

He glances at the farm girl. "If only she were real."

Mr. Mellows continues.

"Anyway, I thought I would challenge myself and start a biotech company. I didn't know any medicine or molecular biology or fancy stuff like that, but I knew people dreamed of cures to nasty diseases, everlasting life and eternal happiness. And that's what biotech was, at that time, anyway: promises. I didn't pick a stereotypical problem like cancer or blindness or diabetes. No sir. Those obvious areas were overcrowded. Competition's a nuisance. I wanted to solve everyday issues that people didn't realize were problems. I settled on a rather silly idea when I think of it now, but it worked, however not as I expected it to. Life is full of curve balls. I wanted to make sweat smell good, appealing, sexy. I know one can simply put on cologne or perfume, but I figured people would like to find a way to make their own sweat appealing rather than cover it up. Vanity, you know. I got $50,000,000 of venture capital from the Miss Universe Foundation, and I established my company in Florida, where they sweat a lot. That was good for another $10 million. At first, I called my company *Sniffme*."

"What happened?"

"Never touched the market I targeted. Had to change the name. Too bad. I liked it. My group of researchers busted their collective ass to find a chemical that could be ingested to make sweat produce a sweet aroma, but nothing really caught on."

"So you lost money?"

"Of course not! We came up with a cream made from crushed cranberries, or was it strawberries? I can't remember. Anyway, it attracted lobsters. Lobsters are a big industry in Florida. Do you know that lobsters have noses? Well, I didn't either, but they do, and they are attracted to good smells, good for them that is. We caught them by the thousands and made a ton of money since everyone loves to eat them. I changed the name of the company to *Taste'em*. I met a scientist who spent his whole life studying lobster noses and he never made a cent. Actually, he begged for money to continue his research by writing grants all the time. People are weird that way. I always went where the money is rather than try to have the money come to me. You can write that down too."

"Yes, sir," said the interviewer as he jotted down *'went where the money is'*.

A musical sound distracts Mr. Mellows. He reaches into the inside pocket of his suit jacket that is hanging on the back of his chair.

"Hello," he says into the cell phone. "Senator Birch's office? I'll wait."

He excuses himself and walks to the far end of the room.

"Yes, Senator, this is Mr. Mellows. Good to hear from you. It was such a pleasure having lunch with you last month. No, no, I have all the time in the world. You're not disturbing me in the least. What's on your mind?'

Silence, except for the low rat-a-tat-tat of syllables flowing from the receiver, and the "uh-ha, yes, umm, interesting, ahh, yes, of course.... mmmmm, absolutely," uttered by Mr. Mellows.

The interviewer waits, looks around and fixates on the picture on the wall. His pupils dilate. He puts down his pen, leans back in his chair and smiles. He looks relaxed for the first time.

"It's a wonderful idea, Ralph. Increasing the visibility of steel will certainly harden the resolve of the American people. You can rely on USC. We must not let terrorism frighten us. Steel is impenetrable, resilient, shiny, strong. It says don't mess with me. A model suburban showcase of steel houses with built in steel furniture powered by the steel-grass lawn says, 'Bring industry back to America'. What an idea! The houses will be bomb proof, tough as...as...won't need repairs. Yes sir, with your support and taxpayers' money, we can do it. What's that? You need cost estimates and a slogan before the President writes his campaign speech next week? No problem. Consider it done. And thank you sir, for your confidence, support, for your great idea. It's an inspiration. America owes you a debt. How about lunch next week, sir? Oh, of course, of course, I understand. We'll lay low. Until later. Bye."

Click.

"Excuse me for another minute, Bob. That's correct, isn't it? Bob? I need to call my deputy."

Mr. Mellows is alert, as before battle. He calls his office.

"Hello. Stacey, get Karl. Quick. Karl? Cancel all meetings for the next two weeks. I don't give a royal damn what we agreed on, just listen. Remember the steel family houses? It's no joke now. Quiet! I told you to listen to me. I'll tell you more later. Damn it, Karl, you're working for me. That's better. Talked to our Senator just now; he swallowed. Who would have guessed? There's big money here. Get Sam and his crew to come up with blueprints for steel houses in which everything is steel: toilets, tables, chairs, everything. Yes. I know it's crazy. Don't argue. Tell the econ guys to gear up for cost estimates. And we need a catchy slogan. See you within the hour. Don't breathe a word of this to anyone. I told you things always work out for the best. It's all about having a positive attitude. You pessimists slay me."

Mr. Mellows replaces the phone in his jacket pocket. He re-buttons his collar and tightens his tie.

The interviewer writes *'positive attitude, don't be pessimistic'* in bold letters and underlines it three times.

"Let's finish up, young man. I've got to leave in a few minutes."

The interviewer is quiet, distant. His gaze turns to the girl milking the cow. "She *is* lovely, isn't she? I mean the scene and everything," he says.

"Yes, indeed. Wouldn't it be nice to live among the aspens, milking cows and chasing butterflies," answers Mr. Mellows, looking past the framed picture to the dead cockroach on the floor.

"You're divorced, Mr. Mellows?" asks the interviewer.

"Yeah, a long time ago. You married?"

"No, no…not… yet," says the interviewer. "Do you have any children?" he asks.

"A daughter, Cynthia. She has two kids…oops, three. I forgot the little one, almost a year old now. Cute little guy, at least when I saw him six months ago. It's hard to get time to go to Chicago. You know what it's like. Anyway, we must close now. Got your story? Business is waiting."

Mr. Mellows puts on his jacket and brushes the dust off the lapel.

"What a spot you picked for the interview! Filthy. I hope it's sold before it deteriorates any more. So, what are you going to say about me?" He looks at his Rolex. The interviewer clips his pen in his shirt pocket. He picks up his notes, pauses and places them back on the table.

"I wrote down what you said, Mr. Mellows."

He gets up and tucks in his shirt, walks to the picture and stares at the pretty girl. "Beautiful, isn't she?"

"That's a bit much, son, but I know what you mean."

"Thanks for the interview, Mr. Mellows. I can't begin to tell you how grateful I am for your time, and your insight. It's been…*useful*."

He moves towards the door without his notes.

"Certainly. Not so fast. Will I see the story before it's published? I don't want any wrong statements to appear."

"The story is on the table, sir. I've got to go before it's too late."

"Wait. Where are you going? Too late for what? Don't you need your notes?"

"Not where I'm going. I've got my eye on this small farm in the country about 100 miles from here, close to where Becky lives. I'm on my way to buy it before someone else has the same idea. It's a great…*opportunity*. Becky loves it. Do you know a cheap place around here where I can buy an engagement ring?" the interviewer asks.

He goes out the door and begins to walk down the stairs.

Mr. Mellows stands alone in the doorway.

"Charles Melinski," he shouts to the interviewer. "My friends call me Chuck. My parents came from Poland. My mother never climbed trees. She died three years ago."

The interviewer stops and looks back over his shoulder. He smiles. Mr. Mellows is standing still at the head of the stairs, his tall frame bearing down on his right leg riddled with nerve pain.

"Thank you, Mr. Mellows," answers the interviewer as he steps out the front door of the building onto the sidewalk.

Mr. Mellows yells at the top of his lungs, "You're an optimist, young man! An *Optimist*, with a capital O!"

A car horn drowns out his voice and the interviewer disappears from sight.

The Doctor Party

I didn't want to give this doctor party, it was my wife Helen's idea, but here I am so I might as well make the best of it. Dr. Kretchmer – Judy, my therapist, who is one attractive (read "sexy"), divorced lady in her thirties – is speaking to Dr. Polimer, a highly regarded gastroenterologist who cured my pre-ulcer three years ago. Polimer, in his early fifties, standing tall (at least 6 feet, 2 inches) as an Olympic athlete, seems to be rattling on like a wind-up toy. Poor Judy must feel trapped. When I last saw Dr. Polimer he went on incessantly about his Arctic trip – a triumph he called it – that accounts for the stuffed, monstrous polar bear some ten feet tall that greets everyone entering his house. No wonder his second wife left him recently.

Judy catches me admiring her from a distance. She is wearing a low-cut, lavender blouse (cleavage included) and a tight (read "clinging"), black leather skirt. Shoes with three-inch heels (at least) wrapped around her foot and ankle with thin straps the exact shade of lavender as her blouse boost her petite size (5 feet, 1 inch, being generous). What a perfectionist! Noticing me noticing her, Judy quickly returns her attention to the gastroenterologist. Psychiatrists know how even a tiny gesture or phrase can spill the beans. That's why she greeted me behind a thick, professional veneer when she arrived. "Hello Mr. Jones. It's very nice to see you again," she had said, extending her hand for a formal shake, and then faced Helen standing beside me, smiled without missing a beat and said, "It's so good to meet you, Mrs. Jones." They had never met before.

I started therapy with Judy two months ago to help me get through depression for being passed over as Partner in my law firm. I have one more chance in a couple of years if I choose to stay, and Judy has given me the confidence to hang in there for the duration.

A couple of weeks ago she said she needed to change my appointments on Tuesdays and Thursdays from my noon lunch break to 6 o'clock, her last session of the day. Okay, that's neither here nor there; in any case, later was more convenient for me. What upset the applecart was that two appointments ago she invited me for a drink after our session. Since her office is an extension of her home, it didn't mean going out. I thought one drink couldn't hurt, and it didn't. Then, after the following therapy session last Thursday, she continued to push the professional barrier: she smiled seductively and said, "I bought a bottle of last year's Chateau Margaux that was on sale. How about testing it together?" I have my weaknesses (I'm not referring to the wine), so I accepted. We downed two glasses on her couch before a dreamy glaze drifted over her eyes like fog rolling in from the quiet sea, and her shoulder-length, fluffy-soft, cocoa-shaded hair that smelled of peaches and cream brushed against my arm when she leaned towards me. How I loved that hazy promise! I was tempted, yes indeed (what red-blooded man wouldn't be?), especially since my twenty-two-year, childless marriage with Helen was in the midst of a mild mid-life crisis. Whatever. I told Judy that I needed to get home for dinner and high-tailed it out of there. Naturally I didn't tell

Helen about this, but I haven't been able to get Judy out of my mind. I was surprised (read worried) when she accepted my invitation for this doctor party. I consider the situation delicate, nothing more, but that's enough.

We are still in the cocktail/appetizer phase of the party, and the guests (about twenty-five in total) are milling about. Not surprisingly, many of the physicians are conversing as if they know one another, or at least have colleagues in common. The spouses and significant others are getting acquainted. The atmosphere resembles my thirtieth high school reunion I attended last month. Being the only lawyer in the room now, I feel like a stranger, like I did in my school days when I had few friends.

Similar genres – academics, writers, doctors, you name it – cohere; they wear the same uniform, so to speak. And they think they are special, one of a kind. How naïve!

Some of the guests haven't arrived yet (read "rudely late"), including: Dr. Walter Wallace (our dentist and his wife); Dr. Alan Wish (our proctologist, a bachelor probably for good reason); Dr. Gerald Leaf (our dermatologist, who insists on being called Greenie), and his handsome partner, Sam; and Michael Schlimer (my barber). Schlimer is not a legitimate doctor, but I invited him anyway because I call him Herr Dr. Professor Schlimer due to his German ancestry. He lives up to that title by focusing on my skull's bumps and blemishes when he cuts my hair.

As retaliation to my inviting my barber, Helen invited her hairdresser, Rob (hairdressers don't have last names), and her manicurist, Dr. (self-bestowed to elevate her status) Gloria Shin, a Chinese immigrant trained in acupuncture. Helen agreed that inviting her facial and waxing people was overkill. She said that all they do is rip out eentsy-bitsy hairs and prescribe moisturizers, which are the real workhorses.

All the doctors (and few honorary "doctors") here have a different knowledge of at least one aspect of Helen or me, or both, than we have of ourselves. If they were to give their views (which, hopefully, they would have the common sense not to) there would be as many versions of us as there are specialists in this room. Here are a few physical/psychological capsules of Helen and me that I imagine might pop into their minds. As for Helen: she has a wonderful complexion, but unfortunately sees only her sickly-looking moles (dermatologist); she misses high frequencies (questionable response at 40 dB at 2 kHz and no response at 40 dB at 4 kHz) in the auditory test, but is too stubborn and vain to get a hearing aid (audiologist); she worries herself sick about her irregular periods and occasional hot flashes and is not aging gracefully (gynecologist); fear of her recurrent bladder infection makes her foolishly avoid even a single glass of wine – what a hypochondriac – she must bore her husband to death (urologist); she has a healthy heart, but who does she think she is kidding by competing in marathons (cardiologist); all the product (read "gunk") she smears on her isn't going to make her look twenty-five again (hairdresser).

It's harder for me to generate a comparable list for myself since I'm burdened with an overwhelming inside view, but here's a sampling of possibilities: he has a deviated septum, but is too stingy or busy to fix it surgically and has rotten priorities (otolaryngologist); I can't believe that he thinks that he can repair his torn medial cartilage in his left knee without surgery – what a misguided dreamer – a delusional superman (orthopedist); if he bit the bullet and replaced his cataracts with lens implants he wouldn't be so damn edgy about driving at night, but he's too dumb, or scared, to listen to me (ophthalmologist); I can't imagine what Judy would say, but I am very curious.

There are certainly a lot more narrow views – or should I say enhanced diagnoses – of Helen and me floating around in this room at the moment, and far more revealing ones at that. But outside views, even from so-called experts, aren't too meaningful without being colored by our inside perceptions that determine who we are. Untangling our several competing natures – the multiple personalities lurking within us and bundled into one package – is as infuriatingly slippery as Heisenberg's uncertainty principle: exposure of one personality trait conceals the others, which await the opportunity to leap onto center stage.

This mélange of complexity drives me back to Helen and her idea three weeks ago to throw this party. What frustrated side of herself is she trying to liberate? The doctor party was a cute idea, but strange. I was against it at first, perhaps because we are going through a rocky period together. Also peculiar, she acted stressed when she suggested it and was evasive when I mentioned that she seemed to be having more doctor appointments than usual. She dismissed the appointments as health-oriented outings. When I probed deeper she deflected by saying, "Just keeping myself in tip-top shape, dear. I'm fine, really." The "really" after "I'm fine" bothered me then, and still does. She's not a "really" type. Was she trying to convince herself or me, or both of us?

The next Sunday at breakfast I was reading the newspaper when Helen said, "Let's have that party, the doctor collection."

At first I didn't like the idea, but I reconsidered when she referred to our doctors as a collection. It gave the idea some unity.

"Yes, Helen," I said, "that's exactly what they are: a collection. Let's assemble the members of our doctor collection. After all, it took us years to accumulate them with great care. They do make a grand bunch, don't they? What a novel idea, to assemble them as one unit compressed in a single room."

Since part of me did think that the party might be fun, or at least interesting, I wasn't happy with my sarcastic response. This was one of those times that I don't like myself very much.

"*Grand bunch?*" she echoed with a tinge of anger mixed with sadness.

Trying to redeem myself I tenderly reached for her left hand (the right was partially paralyzed due to a car accident a couple of years ago, when I was driving too fast for the curve on the slick road). "All I meant by 'grand bunch' was that they are, how to say it, our *life savers*, no? No one does more for us than our doctors." My voice sounded hollow and I didn't even convince myself. Foolishly, I went on. "I hesitate to put lawyers in such a positive light, although they can be useful." Why couldn't I just shut up? "And, honestly, how many real friends do we have, Helen," I continued, "friends that we see as often as our doctors and other providers who take care of our bodies and who we depend upon so much?"

"I wish," Helen said and then paused, the dimple in her chin deepening as it does when she is worried. "*Life savers*, I mean. Maybe."

"Life savers?" I repeated. "What's strange about that? Maybe *what?*"

"What? Nothing. Really."

"*Really*, nothing?" I was confused.

"Nothing."

It's not that I understood what she meant or what was going on in her head, because I didn't, but her distant, lonely voice sounded like a lost little girl and I thought it best to give her some space.

"Okay, let's have that party," I acquiesced.

We mailed out the invitations that afternoon.

When I mentioned to Judy (who had already received an invitation to the party) about Helen being evasive about her health visits, she brushed it off as normal concerns associated with menopause.

"Let's stick to you," she said.

"Okay, fine, but isn't my wife an issue of mine?" I answered.

I thought I might ask Helen's gynecologist, Dr. Harold Lupkin, if anything is going astray with her menopause, but then decided against it. I had promised Helen I wouldn't bring up health matters at the party (but what else to talk about in a roomful of doctors?). In any case, Dr. Lupkin would no doubt invoke patient confidentiality. The inner world of doctors is like the National Security Agency, except with fewer leaks.

And now here we are at the doctor party – Helen's party. I am nursing a glass of red wine and socializing with Dr. Sumner, my podiatrist, who is responsible for the inserts in my shoes. I'm trying my best to be friendly but, in all honesty, he's a bore and I don't know what to say. "My bunion is feeling better," I utter in desperation. When he threatens to take his shoe off to show me *his* bunion, I know it's time to move on. I gulp down the rest of my drink and excuse myself.

As I'm heading for the bar for another glass of wine I spot Helen speaking to our dermatologist, Greenie, who finally arrived. "Nice tan, Helen," I overhear him say. Helen had spent last weekend at the beach with her longtime high school girl friend (why are women friends of women always called girlfriends, while men friends of women suffer from gender deprivation and are reduced to simply friends?).

"I should stay away from the sun, shouldn't I?" Helen says looking guilty.

"Well, yes, that's what I advise my patients – skin cancer, you know – but it has been a beautiful summer to be outdoors."

"That's right, and we don't live forever," Helen mutters as much to herself as to him.

"For sure, at least not in the sun," agrees Sam, Greenie's partner. His skin has the burnt red color of a boiled lobster. Greenie shoots him an angry glance.

The adage, "do as I say, not as I do," comes to mind.

I see Judy on the opposite side of the room still conversing with Dr. Polimer. They have separated a bit from the crowd and her iridescent, lavender blouse makes her shine like a flashlight. I wonder what they are talking about for so long. They're standing quite close together.

"Hi there," says Sally, my dental hygienist, who sneaks up behind me and interrupts my thoughts.

"Sally! I'm so glad you could come."

She is a refreshing change from the other doctors. Sally concentrates on purifying my mouth, making my pearly teeth glitter, rather than stuffing my ears with scary medical warnings or mandates for changing my lifestyle – do more exercise, lose ten pounds, try another prescription for decreasing blood pressure or lowering cholesterol (the *bad*, low density kind). Sally has chipped tartar off my teeth, poked at my gums, and buffed my carnal weapons four times a year for the last twenty years. (I'm prone to plaque build-up.) No one knows my cavernous mouth like her, so when she says, "You have a big mouth," it has an entirely different meaning than that when Helen says it, or when a colleague or adversary say it. Without context, without an inner view that is, words are no more than oil floating on the surface of an ocean of indeterminate depth.

Sally eyes the bowl of chocolate-covered caramels on the coffee table next to me. "They're delicious," she says with a straight face to be polite. She had told me umpteen times to stay away from them (read cavity producers).

"How's that sensitivity on #27?" she asks.

"#27?"

"Yes, you know, the tooth we're watching. Any pain?" Sally likes using the royal 'We'.

"It's fine," I lie.

Decay. Rot. Deterioration. All this reverberates in my mind. Doctors, providers of all types; they are always looking for problems they can fix.

"Good. No more gold for now," she says.

All my fillings are gold for long-term protection against the ravages of time. It's expensive but I look at it as an investment, assuming that gold increases in value as the years progress. I guess I'm an optimist after all.

There's the doorbell. Helen greets Dr. Walter Wallace, the dentist, the last guest to appear. I'm close enough to hear him say, "I'm so sorry to be late. My wife vomited all over my shoes on the way out the door. It must be the twenty-four hour stomach bug that is going around. She's at home resting."

"I'm sorry. I hope everything is all right," says Helen.

"Absolutely," says Dr. Wallace. "I have other pairs of shoes. Not to worry."

What a relief!

Walter Wallace heads straight for Sally, his colleague, and me. "Sorry I'm late, old buddy." He winks at Sally and shakes my hand as if it were an apparatus he uses in the gym.

Old buddy? That's new. It's funny how a relationship depends so much on the environment.

"Glad you could make it, Walter."

"Nice domicile," he says, looking around. "All's well with you and Helen?" Walter swirls his eyes here and there checking out the other guests, apparently no longer interested in how Helen and I are.

"Yes, thank you," I reply, a meaningless answer that feels like an echo from the depths of the crater-like decay I imagine perforating #27. "How about you?" I say, trying to redirect the conversation away from me.

"GREAT!"

I am filled with envy.

"My tennis game is awesome, especially my forehand." He beams. "It feels like butter."

I have no idea how whacking a tennis ball can feel like a fatty spread for bread. Never mind; I haven't played tennis in years.

"I still have trouble with my backhand though," Walter complains.

He swings his arm to show me his stroke and knocks the glass of red wine held by Elaine, our masseuse, onto the Persian rug. Helen was right; she had wanted to serve only white wine that wouldn't stain if spilled. I like red, insisted on it.

"I'm so sorry," Walter tells Elaine, taking in the landscape of her shapely body as he bends down to pick up the glass.

Elaine massages us once a month when she is in town. She often travels with some of her more elite clients.

"No problem. I'll get a refill."

Nothing bothers Elaine. Massaging bodies must be therapeutic. I smile at her.

When Walter is vertical again he scoots back to the tennis court, his true love. "I think I hit the ball too late with my backhand," he says, cheerfully analyzing his game. "My shot often goes wide."

The splotch of red wine that looks like dried blood on the carpet is history to him. I'll still have to deal with Helen about that.

Lucky Walter! I search for wrinkles in his young-looking face and find none, although he is in his sixties and has some twenty years over me. He exudes good health and self-satis-faction: business is booming (patients fill the small torture chambers in his office) and his tennis forehand is thriving. By contrast, I deny having a cavity in #27, have a stain on our expensive rug that is my fault for insisting on red wine, have been passed over as Partner in the law firm and am juggling touchy relations with Helen; and then there's Judy in the wings.

Dr. Polimer is stroking Judy's arm in the far corner of the room and I think her eyes are clouding with that dreamy haze. Maybe I'm mistaken, she's quite far away, but I don't like what I see.

Helen announces that dinner is ready and the herd gravi-tates to the buffet table in the dining room. I take my place at the back of the line of guests. Helen buzzes around being so-cial to everyone, looking nervous, expending energy, although there is no need to do anything but enjoy the party. The ca-terers have everything under control and the guests seem happy enough. I'm getting annoyed with her.

Rob the hairdresser ambles from the living room to the dining room, both arms animated as he lectures my barber, Herr Doctor Professor Schlimer, that long hair is in these days. I overhear Rob saying, "Don't cut short, no, no, no, it's not sexy,"

Schlimer approaches me, looks at my shiny scalp sur-rounded by a short tuft of graying hair and shrugs his shoul-ders. "If you say so, but your customers are quite different from mine," he tells Rob for my benefit.

"Oh, Helen, your hair looks lovely!" Rob says changing the topic with a poorly concealed self-compliment.

Helen forces a smile. "Thank you," she says, moving her lips more than her vocal cords. She told me before the party that her hair is a mess but she's stuck with it, damn it; what could she do?

Helen joins me in the buffet line. I feel sorry for her, but I don't know why. I take her left hand, poor thing. It trembles a bit. She looks sheepishly down at her toes protruding through the oval openings at the end of her new shoes. The fresh, red polish on her toenails is eye-catching next to her silver shoes. I sense that she thinks so too. That makes me happy.

Judy moves closer to the gastroenterologist.

"Are you okay?" Helen asks me. "You look, I don't know, distracted." She then whispers in my ear, "Maybe this party wasn't such a good idea."

The telltale dimple in her chin reflects worry, but what about?

"It's fine," I say, refraining from saying, I told you so. Helen's eyes dart around the room in small jerks. Her gaze lands on a face I don't recognize.

"Are you looking for someone in particular?" I ask.

"Looking for someone?" she repeats. "No, not really."

There's that 'really' again. Maybe she suspects something about Judy, or maybe she is self-conscious in front of this collection of physicians (read "judges") of her body.

"Who is that guy you were looking at a few seconds ago? I've never seen him before."

"Whom do you mean?" she asks.

I point him out. "The guy on the sofa with the gray tie and blue blazer. He's digging into the smoked salmon."

"Oh, he's Dr. Polimer's friend," she says as if she knows him well. "James Ribbons, an oncologist. He divorced a few months ago." After a short pause during which she seems uncomfortable, Helen adds, "Dr. Polimer asked me if he could bring him and I said sure. I guess divorced guys support each other."

An oncologist friend of Polimer's? Recently divorced? Strange that Helen never mentioned him to me? He's pretty good looking.

Does Helen have her Judy, or even more? Did she want this party to tell me something? No, that doesn't sound like Helen.

Judy and Polimer join the line behind us. "Hi, Mr. Jones, Mrs. Jones. Great party," Judy says through her veneer.

It sounds strange for Judy to call me by my last name. I attempt a smile and nod a thank you, wishing I could disappear. Helen tightens her jaw and gives Judy the evil eye (or am I imagining this?), which quickly dissolves into a strained, contorted smile. I hope that the lights are low enough to camouflage the red creeping over my hot cheeks.

Dr. Polimer takes Judy's arm.

"It's hot in here," I say, loosening my tie.

"Really?" says Helen. "Should I lower the thermostat of the air-conditioner?"

"Oh, it's fine, Mrs. Jones." Judy seems perfectly comfortable in this situation that I consider, as I've said before, delicate.

Helen and I load our plates with food: she piles on the salmon and green beans, and I favor the roast beef and French fries. I consider our tastes more complementary than different; together we have a healthy, tasty diet.

"Let's split up for dinner. We need to be sociable hosts," says Helen.

"Okay," I agree.

I head for Elaine, the masseuse, and her date. Her smile is magnetic, and there's an empty chair for me by them.

I keep my eye on Helen to see whom she will join. She walks by the dentist Walter, who is sitting next to Sally the hygienist and her husband and Herr Dr. Professor Schlimer. I hear Walter the dentist saying, "I think Djokovic is unbeatable."

Helen approaches James Ribbons, the mysterious, divorced, oncologist. Ribbons motions Helen to join him and she sits down on the sofa.

Elaine asks me to join them and I sit down next to her. My curiosity is riveted on Helen and Ribbons, while Elaine converses with her date, what's-his-name.

If Ribbons and Polimer are friends, I wonder why they don't sit together at dinner? Neither has a spouse. Maybe Polimer is too absorbed with Judy, who is sitting next to him.

I smell something fishy.

Judy and Polimer slide to the side and sit on two chairs set apart from the other guests. She laughs about something, probably how Mr. Great Hunter slayed a dragon or a fiercer creature.

I enjoy dinner and small talk with Elaine and her date. I learn that he is a bodyguard at the White House, but it doesn't make me feel more secure. After cherry pie and ice cream for dessert, the guests become restless. The party is breaking up.

Helen notices me looking at her and smiles hugely. That's the only way I can describe it: *hugely*. She even waves flirtatiously, like she used to when I courted her many years ago. A carefree air I've always loved has replaced her worried, distant look earlier in the evening. What happened?

James Ribbons gets up, walks to Helen's gynecologist, Dr. Lupkin, and tells him something. Lupkin raises his eyebrows and nods positively. Body language can be louder than words.

Although confused why Helen suddenly looks happy, I find it contagious. For some reason I no longer feel like a stranger in the midst of our doctor collection. I tap my empty wine glass with a knife to attract attention. All eyes point in my direction and I stand up.

"Thank you all for coming tonight. I know that we did not give much advance time between the invitation and the party. To be honest, Helen had the idea to give this party and we jumped right into it. I'm glad we did."

Helen smiles at me from the back of the room.

"We are too," Walter pipes in.

A murmur of approval flutters through the room.

"You see," I pause to crystallize my thoughts, "I believe we all are driven by an abstract fragile future – a fiction that always stays ahead of us – yet it shapes our hopes and dreams and gives meaning to our lives."

A ripple of agreement gives me confidence to continue.

"Well, it is all of you together, our collection of doctors that heal our sores and keep us well, and our other providers – Herr Dr. Professor Schlimer and Elaine and Rob and Sally and the rest of you – I can't mention each of you by name – who care for us and give our fickle, future plans a chance to come true. We depend on you. Helen and I thank you all."

I don't know what else to say so I sit down clumsily, almost missing my chair.

Polimer gets up and breaks the momentary silence by saying: "It's we who thank you for a wonderful evening."

There is a short round of applause. How pleasant that is, even if it's undeserved. Polimer sits down next to Judy.

The guests get up and exchange parting words among themselves. Helen comes and kisses me on the cheek. She looks radiant, as beautiful as I have ever seen her.

"That was so nice," she says. "I love you."

There was no 'really' this time.

"Me too," I say, and mean it, but I feel guilty getting all this credit after having been a curmudgeon about throwing this doctor party.

"Helen, you suddenly seem so relieved or happy, or I don't know. It's so good to see you this way. What happened?"

"Oh, it's Dr. Ribbons. He made my day."

I tense my facial muscles, but Helen doesn't seem to notice.

"He's an oncologist. Remember?"

"Of course."

She continues. "I know I've been evasive, dodging your questions, but I've been so worried and I didn't want to worry you. Actually I think I didn't want to worry myself more by involving you."

"An oncologist? Cancer? What are you talking about?"

"Dr. Lupkin felt a lump in my breast a few days before I suggested this party. He sent me to get a mammogram and then to Dr. Ribbons for a biopsy. I was scared to death. That's what happened to Janice, our neighbor a few years ago, remember? Now she's dead. But it's benign, nothing at all, just a harmless cyst!"

"Oh, my god. You should have told me. I can't believe you didn't."

"I saw my future – our future – disappearing and was terrified. I think I turned to doctors out of, well, maybe desperation. But, isn't it great! I'm healthy! No more doctors for a while. Our future is no fiction. Where did you get that idea anyway?"

I shrug. "I don't know."

I put my arm around Helen to draw her closer. We kiss: our tears, more moist than wet, intermingle.

More small talk and the guests leave, a few at a time. Herr Dr. Professor Schlimer and Walter leave together. "The golf drive has a similar stroke to the tennis backhand, but the ball doesn't move when you hit it so it may be helpful," says Schlimer as they go out the door.

Walter swings his arms as if hitting an imaginary golf ball. "I see what you mean," he says, looking pleased with the suggestion.

Judy leaves conversing with Polimer, that hunter, his long arm around her waist once they are out the door. I don't care at all.

"I didn't picture Dr. Kretchmer – Judy no? – looking like that," Helen says. "She seems nice enough, but she's awfully young and, well, I don't know, pretty snazzy for a psychiatrist. What's the story between her and Polimer?"

"I have no idea."

I tell Helen that it isn't working out with Dr. Kretchmer. "Anyway, I'm going to quit therapy, Helen. I'm feeling a lot better."

Helen looks happy.

"I mean it, Helen. I'll tell Dr. Kretchmer this week, really."

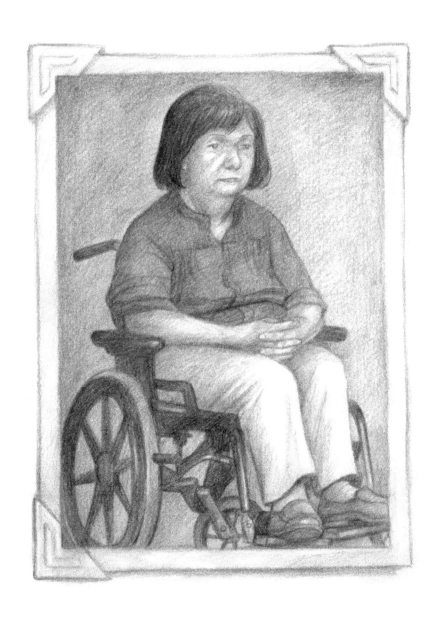

The Miracle of Estelle

For the third time in a row Benjamin didn't have a single matching pair in the cards he held in his hands. His frustration doubled when Estelle flashed her triumphant smile announcing. "Gin!"

"It's not all luck, you know," she said in a self-satisfied voice that rubbed Benjamin the wrong way.

Every Wednesday night, Benjamin accompanied Melinda, his wife of forty-two years, when she visited "poor crippled Estelle." Melinda was more charitable than he was, always willing to help those in need, which is one of traits he loved about her. But, no matter how needy Estelle was, he was irritated watching precious time escape as he played gin rummy with ungrateful and annoying Estelle rather than attend to his unfinished work. The scientific manuscript of his postdoctoral student needed revision, he hadn't prepared his upcoming lecture at Harvard, and his never-ending list of administrative duties for Georgetown University weighed heavily on him.

"Larry didn't come to see me again this week, as if he's too busy to have lunch with his sick mother," Estelle whined, "and my TV flickers so much I can't even see Oprah without getting seasick. The repairman won't come for another week. I'm always last on the list."

"Come on, Estelle," said Benjamin. "Give it a rest."

Melinda shot him a disapproving glance.

Shit, thought Benjamin. I can't win.

"My legs are cold today," Estelle continued, ignoring Benjamin's comment and straightening her back in the wheel chair. She was paralyzed from the waist down and extremely sensitive to temperature changes ever since the onset of a baffling nerve degenerative disease three years ago. She had moved from Chicago to Bethesda to receive medical treatment by a well-known neurologist at the National Institutes of Health. None of her doctors knew if and when this mysterious ailment would stop progressing.

Benjamin asked Estelle about her illness as she dealt another round of cards. "It's God's will," she said, with an astonishing lack of anger that she expressed for other subjects.

"Have courage, Estelle. Maybe Dr. Jensen can help you," said Melinda.

It's not God's will, thought Benjamin. It's got nothing to do with God. It's genetic or viral or maybe something else here on solid earth.

Although Melinda spoke kindly to Estelle, Benjamin wondered what she was really thinking. Two hours ago before coming to play cards that evening, Melinda had said, "Here we go again, dear. It does get tiring, doesn't it?"

He had suppressed asking why they had to keep going to Estelle's every Wednesday night, like robots. Instead he asked, "How do you think God will reward us for our 'Estelle mitzvahs'?"

"Perhaps by a surprise or two, who knows?"

Melinda had learned to side step his sarcasm. Also, the Jewish New Year was in two days, which pacified her. Rosh Hashanah and Yom Kippur were the only religious observances that Benjamin shared with her. He claimed he was a High Holy Day specialist.

Estelle looked more in her late sixties than her fifty-two years. She had aged overnight when her husband abandoned her a few months after she lost the use of her legs. He had claimed it had nothing to do with her disease, but Melinda didn't believe that. Gray roots bridged Estelle's white scalp to thinning, dyed brown hair, her one effort to appear presentable. Since her sickness, she'd neglected caring for home or body. Her clothes were often stained and her shoes dirty; scattered objects, old newspapers and unwashed dishes lay around her small apartment. She had gained at least twenty pounds on her short thick body since she had joined the temple six months ago. Her pudgy face lacked expression, even when complaining, and her tiresome monotone triggered a defensive reaction in Benjamin. However, he fought his instinct to strike back, not always successfully, since he knew she had not attacked him personally. He was doing this principally for Melinda.

Benjamin did have a forgiving nature. He saw Estelle's fingernails coated with dull red, peeling polish as worn weapons that had lost their threat, unlike claws of a predator, calming his desire to snipe at her. It was not what she said or her appearance that irked him most, but rather it was her certainty about everything. Always the academic scientist, he rebelled against opinions stated as facts or beliefs not supported by evidence.

Benjamin walked into temple the following Friday morning clutching his prayer book but thinking about the lecture he was missing at the university on stem cells. "Nice day," he said to Melinda, then gazed at the cloudless blue sky.

"Yes," she answered as she passed the entrance of the temple.

As the Rosh Hashanah service started and the empty seats disappeared, he noticed a thin diagonal scratch in the back of the polished pew before him. He leaned forward to see a tiny heart at its base etched into the wood from the same sharp point. LN + PDU were printed in pencil underneath the heart. He speculated these as initials of imaginary people Lynn Nussbaum + Peter Denon Ukevitch. Why not? Everything we hear in Temple is imaginary. Then he wondered whether 'Lynn' or 'Peter' made the scratches, and whether they really loved each other, or maybe someone just imagined phantom people like he did to entertain the old guys, like him, doing their duty on Rosh Hashanah.

"Look, young lovers," he whispered to Melinda as he pointed to the heart.

"Shhh. Not so loud." She abruptly turned the page of her prayer book and he got the message.

"Rise as the Arc is opened," commanded the new rabbi, who had just replaced Rabbi Magnum on his retirement. Young Rabbi Fraenkel was the future: the changing of the guards to continue the never-ending cycle that kept treading back on itself.

"Please be seated," the rabbi said after the Arc was closed.

"All rise and turn to page 93 in your prayer book. Let us read responsively," said the rabbi a little later.

O Lord, You have been our refuge
From generation to generation.

The rabbi motioned for the congregants to be seated again.

Up and down, up and down, won't need to go to the gym today, thought Benjamin. A trickle of sweat slid down his cheek. He wiped off the perspiration with his fingers and rubbed his eye with his knuckle. The September heat was oppressive in Bethesda.

Practicing his speed-reading skills Benjamin skimmed forward in his prayer book, blocking out the background voice of the rabbi.

The Lord is King, The Lord was King,
The Lord shall be King throughout all time.

He was baffled why so many smart people repeated such nonsense over and over. If they meant the King is Nature, why didn't they say so? If they meant there is a supernatural force out there protecting people or directing events…well…how could anyone really believe that? He questioned for the umpteenth time what he was doing here, and then reminded himself of Melinda's devotion and his vows so many years ago "… in sickness and in health, until death do us part."

His leg touched hers and she smiled.

"Please rise."

Up again. Benjamin noticed strangers of all ages studying their books, standing as instructed, like soldiers, except for the girl in the stroller next to her young parents. Benjamin looked down at his feet and wiggled his toes. Obedient little fellows, he told himself, feeling disconnected from his body. I guess we all do what we're told, he thought, becoming strangely angry at his toes.

His mood mellowed as the congregants' joined the Cantor's deep voice in song and he saw Melinda swaying with the tune. The age-old melodies had become familiar over the years that he had attended Rosh Hashanah services with Melinda and were separate in his mind from the mechanical religious observances. It was as if the music and prayers, although under the same roof, had little to do with one another.

Benjamin tried to sing along with Melinda and the rest of the congregation but couldn't maintain the melody for more than a few moments, adding to his frustration at the service. He had difficulty pronouncing and didn't know the meaning of the Hebrew words, which often made him feel as an outsider, instead of imagining, as he usually did, that the others were chained within. It was as if he had not earned entrance into the privileged inner sanctum of Jews, or that birthright was insufficient to join this holy setting. Yet, he didn't feel rejected either. Rather, he felt that he had an illicit membership to an exclusive club.

A sense of estrangement was not new to Benjamin. He was the first American citizen of his family, having been born in New York a few months after his French mother and Russian father emigrated from France just in time to escape Hitler. His parents neither sent him to Hebrew school nor attended services themselves as he grew up assimilating new customs in a foreign land that they now called home. He was an American/European/non-observant Jewish refugee raised in a peaceful country. He felt no more a ritualistic Jew clinging to past traditions than he a felt a target of Jewish persecution and Nazi extermination. Singing itself was difficult for him personally as well. His father was a musician, but Benjamin was tone-deaf and self-conscious when he sang. He imagined himself a deficient mutant when singing among others. His lips attempted to form words without sound for the rest of the song.

Benjamin, bored, started thinking about Estelle. He assumed that she was at the service and wondered who brought her to the temple or where she was sitting. He hoped Melinda wouldn't ask her to join them for lunch after the sermon, a tradition he had with her every year. Also, he didn't want to be stuck with Estelle that afternoon. He was looking forward to catching up on his work. He scanned the crowd looking for her but didn't see her anywhere. The wheelchair should have been easy to spot.

"Where's Estelle?" he asked Melinda.

She shrugged. "I don't know."

Benjamin's attention was diverted to the Cantor starting his journey up the aisle carrying the Torah. Many congregants shuffled along their rows in his direction. A gray-haired man eager to reach the Torah maneuvered across Benjamin and Melinda's row to reach the aisle. The end of his tallit, tassels dangling, was clutched in his fingertips and his arm extended towards the on-coming Torah. A changing flux of hands holding either prayer books or edges of tallits danced around the ancient Torah as it proceeded down the aisle. Golden rings, jeweled bracelets and cuff links screamed opulence while the act begged humility. No icons allowed, said the Jews. Yet, Benjamin saw them tied to ritual and the Torah. Were those not icons of a kind?

The books and tallits touched the Torah, ever so lightly, so lovingly, so reverently, and quickly receded to the lips of their owners for spiritual nourishment, a taste of honey.

Benjamin recoiled from the programmed bonding between Torah and Jew. He found the subservience as unpalatable as the evangelists on television Sunday mornings praising Jesus Christ. Save for the rare scholar, why *kiss* a book or cloth after it touched a scroll that he had neither read nor understood? Why use lips; why *kiss*? It has nothing to do with the passion of lovers with moist lips, open, or with lips nuzzling on an infant's neck, or even with the social masquerade of lips smacking air as cheeks brushed past each other. To Benjamin, this Jewish kiss meant, "I'll obey, I'm yours," less like the fearful kissing of the Godfather's ring than the obsequious kissing of the Pope's. He would have preferred to *touch* the silver case of the Torah with his fingers. But, it was so distant, he thought, to touch but not to feel, so unsatisfying, like the *near* contact of a gentleman's lips meeting a lady's hand.

He could not bring himself to extend his arm, but didn't touch the Torah and touch his lips. Apart from the hypocrisy for him, it was an ostentatious performance, like yelling

"Bravo!" at a concert, to stand out as a connoisseur, a true music lover, one who belongs, yet plays no instrument and cannot sing in tune. He looked at the other congregants touching and kissing, avoiding each other's eyes to make it all more sincere. The bowing, the swaying, the yarmulke and tallit, the reaching to touch the Torah in a mass frenzy – all distasteful public displays and badges of belonging – thought Benjamin. Was all that necessary?

What about the others, like himself, who were born members of the so-called Chosen People (chosen by whom?), but chose to look forward, not backward, and settled with being a member of the human race, despite their flaws, the product of eons of evolution, rather than being confined to an encapsulated group, special, claiming a singular privilege to misery? Every year it was the same: he watched, a peeping Tom, a Jewish peeping Tom, watching Jews.

But then other nagging questions rattled around in Benjamin's mind and confused him. *Am I* participating in earnest? I'm here, aren't I? I'm always here on Rosh Hashanah. I'm a Jew with a Jewish wife celebrating the New Year with other Jews. Don't people need family? Don't I? I am a product of history as everyone else here. He responded to the songs, rose to the call, read, on cue, that God is one, all-powerful, benevolent, never to be doubted, always to be honored. Did it really matter that he did not believe the voice of certainty in the prayer book, or that his hand was not among those seeking the Torah, or that his lips were not brushing against the object made holy by contact with the Torah, or that he was an Atheist, with a capital A? He was there, willingly, wearing his talllit and yarmulke. Doesn't the uniform define the person? Wouldn't a person camouflaged in a white sheet and sporting a pointed hat listening to the Grand Wizard be branded a member of the

Ku Klux Klan whatever his private beliefs? Do thoughts trump actions? No. The messy informal appearance of a research scientist, like himself, was part of that person. He was *there* all right. With Melinda. If a modern day Gestapo invaded the temple at that very moment he would be incarcerated with her and the others.

He re-centered his light brown yarmulke (left over from the Bar-Mitzvah of Danny Shapiro, a friend of his daughter) and re-arranged his white and blue tallit to cover the full expanse of his shoulders, which sagged a bit with advancing years. He gazed at the Cantor walking along the aisle at the far left of the chapel heading back to the bima. Few remained around the Torah, a touch here, a tap there, kiss, kiss, the bees quieting as the hive prepared for the next phase.

Various members of the congregation went to the bima to read their assigned words of Hebrew, a plea was made to buy Israel bonds, more chants, up, down, yawns, the chapel door opened, closed with congregants taking breaks to sip water from the fountain or relieve themselves or maybe just chat with a friend and express condolences for a sick family member, or congratulations for a promotion, whatever, and then back to the sanctuary, the rituals, the service that put all lives on hold for the day, playing guiltless hooky from work, with pride and comfort and sense of community. It was their tribe, after all, for centuries, and it was Rosh Hashanah.

Happy New Year! Last year was wonderful, a blessing. Touch wood; *touch* again. Next year in Jerusalem! Maybe next year all our dreams will come true. Maybe. *Maybe.*

Benjamin pondered what thoughts filled the minds of the other congregants at this very instant. His six-foot, four-inch frame allowed him to see over the heads in front of him (except for one very ugly purple hat that blocked his view) and it all looked ordinary, a group of people observing the Jewish New Year, as expected of them. His thoughts turned more scientific and he wondered how many of the strangers in this holy chamber would be dead next year, how many malignant tumors were in the room, how much anxiety, how many would hear devastating news within the week about their health, or their jobs, or their children (god forbid). Then he gave himself a break and wondered how many orgasms would they generate today, and how many conceptions, wanted and unwanted, occurred last night?

This scene may have appeared commonplace, but so do tragedy and ecstasy from afar. A room full of people is high drama, he thought, the stuff of literature and life, just notice, think, *imagine*. His thoughts returned to the contradictions of authenticity: was it mind or body, beliefs or actions? Could he be religious and not religious at the same time? Who wins the battle of competing truths?

And then Benjamin heard a human voice that put aside his tiresome conflicts. It had a wondrous quality, like the first chirp of a bird at dawn. The tapestry of suits, dresses, jewelry, hair shades, scarves, the background of people that had distracted him, surrendered to the feminine melody so fine that it sounded like a single violin string caressed by a bow containing a hair plucked from the head of a child-angel. The voice was not powerful or tutored like that of a soprano's trained for opera, but free like air filling the sanctuary, entering his body with every breath.

Benjamin's invisible shield melted. He glanced at Melinda beside him and took her hand in his. She squeezed his fingers. He closed his eyes and imagined the ebb and flow of tides in a calm sea where life originated. His face relaxed and the creases lining his forehead disappeared. The warmth of that single voice made him shiver in the September heat. It didn't matter anymore whether there was a God that was good or powerful or existed at all. With Benjamin's hand in Melinda's in his private dark space of closed eyes, there was no inner or outer group; that one human voice kidnapped his conflicts.

Benjamin leaned close to Melinda and asked, "Who is singing?"

"I don't know," she said.

"Where is it coming from?"

"The choir, I think."

Benjamin scrutinized each person within the choir standing at the front of the chapel. No lips were moving, yet the spellbinding voice. He searched the congregants for the woman who sang, but found none. Again he examined the choir carefully, and then he noticed a space between two women standing in the second row. A metallic flash caught his attention. He squinted and thought he may have identified the source of the voice. He shifted in his seat trying to see her more clearly.

Estelle! Yes, he was sure now. She was trapped in her wheelchair as usual. Her eyes were shut and except for her lips, she was perfectly still. Oh my, Estelle! Benjamin wondered whether she plucked the notes out of the heavens and blew them gently to the audience. This was not Estelle's gin-rummy voice Benjamin heard on Wednesday nights.

The older couple in front of him stopped whispering to each other. The rabbi stopped fiddling with his tallit. Even the baby stopped fidgeting in the stroller. The occasional coughs, the muffled chatter, the turning of pages, the restlessness all ceased. This voice was for listening, not joining or interrupting. It demanded no action and claimed no certainty; it was from another world where understanding came simply from being a part of it. Estelle was singing purely and beautifully. That was all. The preaching of the rabbi, the chanting of the cantor and the rituals of the congregants seemed insignificant. Benjamin's desire to prove his identity to himself or to anyone else dissolved. He imagined symphonies playing in the heads of the deaf. And then as Estelle's voice had permeated the sanctuary, it eased to its conclusion without fanfare.

A solemn hush lingered. There was no applause, no bow. There would be no headline in tomorrow's newspaper: "Estelle Changes Lives: Jews Honor the New Year". A lady in a wheelchair had sung her song to a congregation at Rosh Hashanah. But Benjamin knew that he would carry this sound with him when the sun set that evening.

Rabbi Fraenkel broke the magic of the moment with a mundane sermon about the importance of retaining Jewish roots through observance.

After the service he saw Estelle being wheeled to the lobby by her son Larry. She was criticizing him for pushing the wheelchair recklessly. Benjamin saw that her purple-red lipstick, too heavily applied, spread unevenly beyond the boundaries of her parched lips.

"Estelle," said Melinda. "That was wonderful. I had no idea… what a voice you have."

"Yes, yes, absolutely, amazing. I didn't know. You never said anything," added Benjamin.

"Thanks," she said. "God, it's hot in here. Do they think we're made of plastic or something?"

She laughed coarsely, as usual, starring straight ahead with her deadpan bug-eyes. Her blue sweater was rumpled and her canvas shoes stained. Her earrings were too small for her big ears, and she was wearing a gauche necklace with large blue, glass beads.

Such a mess, thought Benjamin. She was as obnoxious as ever. Just seeing her in her wheelchair made him shy away. That her divine voice had returned to some mysterious place within her haunted him.

"Good singing," said a passing congregant as he raced out the front door. "Happy New Year!"

"Yes," said Larry. "Good singing."

Benjamin moved close to Melinda as they left the Temple. He removed his yarmulke and tallit; the service was over; the New Year had officially begun. Larry wheeled his mother out behind them. Benjamin turned as bright sunrays filtered through the leaves of a nearby tree and brightened Estelle's face. A slight breeze made shadows dance on her cheeks. He took a step in her direction and touched her arm.

"Thanks, Estelle. We'll see you next Wednesday?" he said.

He could not be sure, but hoped that the small movement of Estelle's lips was a smile.

"I guess," she said. "Wednesday."

Melinda took Benjamin's arm and they headed together towards their favorite small Greek restaurant where they always ate lunch after Rosh Hashanah services to usher in the Jewish New Year.

About the Author

During his 50-year career at the National Institutes of Health, Joram Piatigorsky, a life-long writer, has published some 300 scientific articles and a book, *Gene Sharing and Evolution* (Harvard University Press, 2007), lectured worldwide, received numerous research awards, including the prestigious Helen Keller Prize for vision research, served on scientific editorial boards, advisory boards and funding panels, and trained a generation of scientists.

Presently an emeritus scientist, he is on the Board of Directors of The Writer's Center in Bethesda, has published essays and short stories in the literary journals, *Lived Experience* and *Adelaide Literary Magazine*, a novel, *Jellyfish Have Eyes* (IPBooks, 2014) and a memoir, *The Speed of Dark* (Adelaide Books, 2018). He collects Inuit art and blogs about science, writing and art at JoramP.com.

He has two sons, five grandchildren, and lives with his wife in Bethesda, Maryland. He can be contacted at joram@joramp.com.